INKED

TT KOVE

ARCTIC CIRCLE PRESS

PROLOGUE

I glared at the car parked outside of our shabby flat. Mum was *entertaining* again? Couldn't she stay alone for a single day before pulling someone new?

It wasn't like I'd held out any hope for this particular day. She'd never given a rat's arse before, but turning eighteen... It was kind of a big deal. I'd hoped, *wished*, that she could've at least acknowledged it.

I should've known better.

She'd never acknowledged any of my other seventeen birthdays—not as far as I could remember, anyway.

I desperately wished I could afford to move out, but I was still doing my A-levels, and I spent all my time doing the very best I could so I would be able to move out come summer. I needed good results on all my A-levels so I could get a good job.

Maybe hairdressing wasn't the most lucrative career, or the one I'd need the best grades in A-levels to get, but I wasn't taking any chances. The better my A-levels, the better my chances were of getting hired as a trainee in a good salon.

No matter what, I would leave my mum's house, which was something I'd been waiting to do for forever.

I could hear shouting even before I opened the front door, and my spirits fell further.

Mum usually left me alone whenever she had men over, and as long as I kept to my room and had my music on, I was kept from being traumatised. But if she was already in a screaming match with today's bloke, then there would be no peace for me.

I almost didn't go inside, but it wasn't like I had anywhere else to go, so I had no choice.

"You have no bloody right to be here!" Mum's screams came from the direction of the living room.

I hoped to avoid her and sneak into my room, where I could plug in my earphones and avoid the entire fight. It must be a record, even for her, to already be fighting with whatever new man she'd brought home.

Usually around this time they were busy in bed.

"I have every right to be here now. He's eighteen today, which means you can't keep me away anymore!"

And just like that, I realised that this wasn't one of Mum's many shags, and that their screaming match was about *me*.

I abandoned my attempt to sneak off to my room and instead tip-toed over to the living room doorway.

Mum and the male stranger faced each other in the middle of the floor, and I could see both their profiles. Mum was livid, while the man looked frustrated, but also determined.

"You can't deny me this. He's eighteen. You have no say in his life anymore. If he wants to see me, you can't stop him. You can't stop *me* anymore." The man pointed a finger in Mum's face and she swatted angrily at it.

"You really think he'll want anything to do with you, John? You've been MIA for his *entire* life."

"Because of you! Because you've kept me away, refusing to let me to see him!" The frustration was bleeding away from the man now, and it was replaced by livid anger. "You're a spiteful bitch, and you've managed to keep me away all these years, but not anymore. From today on, it's *his* choice."

I stared at him, realisation dawning on me slowly.

This was my *father*.

My actual *father*.

All I knew about my biological father was that he'd left when I was little. Mum had never wanted to talk about him, except to badmouth him, and I'd eventually learned not to ask.

And now here he was.

He was here for *me*.

I must've made a sound, or moved; I didn't know which. All I knew was that they both turned to me.

Mum's eyes narrowed, while the man's eyes widened.

I knew I stared, and I knew my mouth was slightly open and that I must look completely ridiculous, but that was my *dad* standing there, staring right back at me. I couldn't remember him, had never known what he looked like. I'd never thought I'd *ever* be able to meet him.

"Kian." He took a step forward and I took swift note of the fact that I had his eyes and nose and cheekbones. I basically looked like a male version of Mum, just smaller, kinder and even more effeminate than her, but those features... those were from *him*.

I swallowed heavily.

I couldn't move, I couldn't speak.

What was I supposed to do?

My *dad* was right there. Alive, well, and he seemed to actually *want* to meet me. I had no idea what to say in this situation.

"Get the fuck out of my house, the both of you," Mum snapped, bringing me out of my shocked state.

"What?" Now I stared at her, shocked for an entirely different reason.

"You're eighteen now." Her voice was cold. Her eyes were even colder. "You can provide for yourself. You're no longer welcome here."

My eyes burned.

You will not cry.

You will not *cry.*

"I have nowhere to go, Mum."

"Go with him." She jerked her head in his direction. "He apparently wants you." Now she jerked a thumb at him too. "Get your stuff and get the hell out." With that said, she stalked away into the kitchen. The door slammed shut behind her so hard that the glass in it quivered.

I flinched, then stood rooted to the spot, clutching at the strap of my shoulder bag as I stared at the closed door.

Now what am I supposed to do?

A hand on my shoulder startled me into movement, and I turned back to stare at the man who was my *father*.

"Come with me, Kian," he said in a low voice. "Please. Come with me."

I glanced from the closed door to him—my dad.

He seemed genuine in his plea, but there was more than that, he was *begging* me to come with him. There was desperation in his eyes, and his hand still clutched at my shoulder as if he didn't want to let me go.

"I'm gay," was what came out of my mouth.

I'd never told my mum, because she'd never given a shit, but it wasn't hard to tell. Still, if he wanted to get to know me, then that was a big part of who I was.

He smiled tightly. "I don't mind."

And I believed him.

The tightness seemed to be more about the fact that we were still in my mum's living room, and he seemed anxious to leave it. "Truly, I don't."

I nodded slowly. "Okay, then."

His eyes lit up a bit. "You'll come with me?"

I clutched my shoulder bag tighter. "I don't have any other choice, do I?" I took several steps back, out of the room. "I'm not welcome here anymore."

"You're welcome with me. With us."

I'd started to turn towards my bedroom door, but now I faced him again. "Us?"

"Me, my wife, and my son. My second son." His

smile lost a bit of the tightness now, though it was still there. His hands clenched at his sides.

Is he nervous?

But nervous about meeting me or going head-to-head with my mum? Maybe both.

I opened my bedroom door and headed inside.

He followed hesitantly.

I glanced around at what little I had. It wasn't much, but I still didn't know how to get everything with me.

I found a bag in my closet and stuffed all my clothes in it. I had too few as it was, and since I didn't have much money, it was necessary for me to bring all of them with me.

"We can go back and get everything later," he suggested, seeing my predicament. "We can get some boxes to pack everything in."

"I'm not sure she'll let us in if we leave now and then come back," I murmured.

He looked around, assessing. "Then we'll get everything with us. We'll just put it all in the back seat."

I gazed at him from under my fringe. "You really want me to stay with you?"

He nodded quickly. "You're my son; of course I want that. I didn't get the chance to be a part of your life for so long, but now that you're of age, I very much want to be."

I chewed on my bottom lip. "She kept you away all these years?"

His expression turned grim. "When I left her, I didn't have a job. I didn't have anything. She fought me for full custody and she won. From then on, I wasn't allowed to see you or contact you in any way, and whatever I tried, she rebuffed."

I turned my head away so he couldn't see my face. "Doesn't surprise me." Mum had never cared about him—so it didn't surprise me at all that she'd only kept me out of spite.

"I'm so sorry." He came further into the room.

The room I'd grown up in. The walls were littered with posters, of hair or make-up or half-naked blokes. They didn't hold any particular value, though, so leaving them behind wouldn't be terrible.

We got everything I wanted to keep out in his car.

I left some small knick-knacks, as well as the posters, and I didn't doubt for a second she'd throw everything away the minute I was out of the flat.

I looked back once I was ready to get in the passenger seat. We'd lived in that flat for as long as I could remember. It was my childhood home, even if it didn't hold many good memories.

"How about we go out to eat now, just the two of

us?" He suggested from the other side of the car. "Then you can come home with me, and meet my wife and your little brother afterwards."

I turned my head to focus on him. "Why not go meet them right away?" I asked, puzzled.

He smiled slightly. "Selfish reasons. Now that I've finally met you again, I want you to myself for a bit."

The words warmed me and I ducked my head as my eyes started burning again.

"Dinner sounds good." I slid into the car, and he got settled in the driver's seat as well. I watched his hands grip the wheel. "I don't know what to call you."

His hands tightened for a second, then relaxed. "If Dad is too weird for you, you can just call me John."

I chanced a glance up and he smiled. "Okay." I returned the smile then gazed out my window when he backed the car out of the parking space. "John."

Whatever I called him, there was no denying what he was—he was my dad, and he hadn't abandoned me like I'd spent most of my life believing. He'd been kept away by my own mother, which was yet another reason not to miss her, to get away from her.

I have my dad back.

I couldn't have got a better gift for my birthday.

CHAPTER 1

"*A*re you sure you want to do this?" I looked at my best friend inquiringly, wanting to be the voice of reason before she did something she could potentially regret.

Chloe all but vibrated besides me. "I am so ready; you have no idea!" She nudged me with her shoulder, grin wide. "Stop worrying so much. You should do it yourself. Your skin would look so good with some colour on it to match your hair."

I rolled my eyes as we stopped beside the tattoo shop. There was a light on inside, but the door itself was locked. The sign was turned to *closed*.

Chloe wasted no time knocking. She even did that cheerfully today. She'd been all excited about getting her first tattoo all day.

I wasn't entirely certain on how she'd got me to go with her. I had better things to do after work than watch her sitting in a chair for hours, getting a design tattooed on her body. But somehow she'd talked me into it, and so there I was.

The lock clicked and the door opened, the bell above it ringing in the process.

I turned—and found myself face to face with the most handsome bloke I'd ever laid my eyes upon.

His hair was black and cut in a short faux-hawk. His face was square and masculine and altogether well-proportioned. His eyes were a steely grey and framed by dark lashes, and I literally felt my heart skip a beat as I looked into them.

I lowered my gaze slowly, taking in soft-looking lips that I wouldn't mind kissing, a toned chest clad in a really tight tee, tattooed arms bared for me to ogle, strong thighs clad in form-fitting jeans that clearly showed off the bulge in his crotch.

Oh, bloody hell.

"Silver." Chloe cut in front of me. She hugged him, he hugged her back, and they seemed entirely too familiar with each other.

She hadn't said anything to me about knowing the bloke who was going to tattoo her and I found myself ticked off.

I had no right feeling that way, rationally, seeing

as I didn't know the man and Chloe was in a relationship. She was here to get a tattoo designed by her girlfriend, after all.

Still, they did seem very familiar with each other.

"Thanks for doing this." Chloe smiled brilliantly up at him. "I really appreciate it."

"No problem." His voice slid like an intimate caress down my spine, even if it hadn't been directed at me. It was deep, masculine. "Come in." He stepped out of the way and Chloe didn't hesitate in brushing past him on her way in.

I followed her more slowly.

I couldn't help but look up at the bloke—Silver?— when I walked past him, and our eyes locked.

He smiled, showing off straight, white teeth, and I felt like I might just melt into a puddle right there at his feet.

"I brought some moral support. I hope you don't mind."

"Not at all." His gaze travelled down my body, then up, until our eyes locked again. If that wasn't a show of blatant interest, I didn't know what was.

He turned to close and lock the door again and I couldn't help but take in his strong, wide back and tight arse.

I hadn't been this instantly taken with someone at first sight in... well, ever.

And certainly never with someone who expressed a clear interest back.

It was exhilarating.

Too bad Chloe was there.

Or maybe it was a good thing; her presence stopped me from jumping him and ripping his clothes off right then and there.

"Everything's ready." He turned away from me to face Chloe. "Just sit down, take off your blouse, and let's get started."

Chloe didn't waste any time doing as she was told. After throwing her blouse over the reception desk, she pulled her long, black hair into a ponytail then went further into the studio to sit down in the big, black leather-upholstered chair.

Silver walked past me, his arm brushing against my side lightly.

I wasn't sure if it was accidental or on purpose, but either way, I liked it.

He sat down on a stool, blocking my view of Chloe.

I didn't mind, because I had a perfect view of his splendid backside. Suddenly, going with Chloe to get a tattoo had turned from a prospect of utter boredom to sporting a semi-boner. But with this kind of eye-candy to admire, who could blame me?

"Go look at yourself in the mirror. If you don't

like the placement, now's the time to shout out. There'll be no way back otherwise." He swivelled around on his chair, startling me as I was suddenly faced with his front.

I saw Chloe get up off the chair from the corner of my eye, but otherwise my attention was all on the bloke in front of me.

"Do you have any tattoos?" His voice was low and his head tilted curiously to the side.

"No. I don't."

"He wants one," Chloe helpfully shot in. "He just doesn't know what and where."

Thrilling goosebumps erupted down my spine as he took me in from top to bottom again. That look was intense. It was almost like I could feel it caress me. "I've got some suggestions as to placement."

Oh, blimey.

I drew my lower lip in between my teeth and bit down on it. I was getting *so* hard. From nothing but his appearance and the look he was giving me. It shouldn't be allowed, or even possible, but it was. My dick swelled behind my fly, and I thanked a god I didn't even believe in that my jeans were so tight that they kept it firmly in place.

"It looks great, Silver." Chloe dropped back down on the chair. "Do your magic."

Silver chuckled, the sound also going straight to

my groin. He snapped on a pair of latex gloves before readying his equipment.

I took a few steps to the side, wanting to see what he was doing. Maybe watching him tattoo her would get my own arousal out of my mind.

Except it didn't.

Looking at Silver's hands, at the way his long fingers held the tattoo needle, how they worked it over the lines of the pin-up woman stencil, how they slid over Chloe's pale skin and cleaned up the residue ink… it was so erotic that I had to look away.

"I'm just going to—" I motioned behind me, then disappeared into the front before I had to clarify what exactly it was I was going to do.

I was supposed to be so-called moral support, but I couldn't watch Silver tattoo anymore, unless I wanted to completely embarrass myself.

I busied myself looking at the various pictures hanging on the wall. Some were of real people, showing off their tattoos, others were simple tattoo designs. I went over to the waiting area, which consisted of two settees. Books were scattered on the table, all with tattoo designs. I browsed through them, more interested in getting my thoughts off Silver tattooing and the arousal he had caused than the designs themselves.

"Kian!" Chloe's shout brought me out of my

thoughts a while later. The designs had turned out to be interesting after all.

"What?" My gaze instantly made its way to Silver's fingers as I went back. They worked the needle deftly along Chloe's upper arm.

"Should it be in colour?" She looked down at him working, too. "Quinn's original version was in black and white, but wouldn't it look good in colour, you think? More vibrant, like."

I shifted my focus to stare at her blankly. "It's up to you, innit? If you want an opinion, maybe you should ask your girlfriend? She's the one you're doing it for."

"I can colour it another day." Silver didn't take his eyes off his work as he spoke. "If you decide that that's what you want. It's no problem."

Chloe nodded. "You're an angel."

"Hardly." He scoffed, and then sat back on the stool. He swiped the paper over Chloe's skin, wiping away ink and blood. "There. All done for now."

It looked good.

Really good.

I would've never wanted a pin-up girl on my own skin, but if I had been a lesbian or a straight man, I would've seen the appeal.

It looked good on her, anyway, and I was sure

Quinn would love to see her own design on Chloe's skin.

I grinned at her. "It looks great."

Chloe beamed at me as Silver finished up by covering the tattoo with ointment, then clean film. At least I assumed that was what it was.

Silver told her how to take care of the tattoo for the coming days, but I wasn't listening to what he said. I was too busy staring at his profile and enjoying the sound of his deep voice.

He was so bloody *gorgeous*.

"Quinn should be off work soon." Chloe stood and pulled her blouse back on, being careful with her wrapped-up tattoo. "Again, thank you so much for doing this." She hugged Silver tight, then came over and kissed me on the cheek. "And you, thank you for coming with me. I'll see you at work tomorrow!"

"Wha—" I turned around in surprise as the front door slammed shut after her, wondering just what had happened.

Chloe had left me there, all alone in the tattoo shop with a bloke I wanted nothing more than to pounce on.

"I have a confession to make."

I turned back around at Silver's low voice. "What?"

"I kind of bribed Chloe." He finished putting

away all his equipment, then put all his focus on me. He leaned back against the counter, arms crossed over his chest, which made his already-tight tee stretch even more over his broad shoulders.

"Bribed her?" I shook my head slightly, not understanding what he was getting at.

"I told her I'd do her tattoo for free if she brought you with her."

I blinked. "Um, why?"

He chuckled, but judging by the way his gaze suddenly couldn't meet mine, it was obvious he was at least a little on edge.

He's nervous.

"Why could I possibly want to spend time with you?"

It clicked for me and my heart sped up.

Silver wanted to spend time with me.

Me.

But…

"How do you know who I am? I have no idea who you are." It might be rude to say, or admit, but it was true. I'd never seen him before in my life.

"Yeah, I'd imagine you don't." He looked at a spot above my head. "I've known Chloe for a while now; she's related to my best friend, who also happens to be my flatmate. I've been to the salon several times. She always cuts my hair. And you've never so much as even looked at me."

I swallowed heavily. "I-I'm sorry." He'd known who I was for some time and he'd wanted my attention. It was... the most flattering thing I had ever heard.

"Don't apologise, it's not your fault." He smiled slightly.

"But I am. I do. If I'd seen you—Trust me, I wouldn't have forgotten you." Oh no, I certainly wouldn't have forgotten that face or that body or those tattoos. He was a wet dream.

His steel grey eyes locked with mine. "Oh, really?"

"Yes." I stared back. "You could've just got my attention, you know."

"Don't I already have it?" One corner of his mouth quirked up into a wry smile.

I blinked again, surprised, then slowly returned his smile. "Yeah." I felt both flustered and flattered all at once at his interest. I was pretty sure my face was beet red. "Yeah, you do. You had it from the moment you opened that door."

I took several steps forward, closer to Silver who still leaned back against the counter.

I might sound like an idiot, an insecure idiot at that, but I couldn't help but ask what was on my mind. "Why me? What is it about me that caught your attention?"

He yanked me close so fast that only a small gasp managed to escape me. "I don't know." His voice was husky. *Sexy.* "Maybe it was your hair. It was a bright green the first time I saw you. Very catching, for sure." Silver tangled one hand in said hair, which was currently black with rainbow-dyed tips. "Or maybe your pretty face." His free hand cupped the side of my cheek, his thumb rubbing softly over my lips.

I didn't know what to say.

I could only stare into the steel-grey eyes and think that I'd never experienced anything like this.

Silver used his grip on my hair to tilt my head further up, and in the next second I was being firmly kissed.

I wrapped my arms around his waist, pressing myself up against him as I kissed him back with all I had.

He was a good kisser.

I went from a semi to rock-hard in no time, and I couldn't seem to get close enough to him.

The brief thought that I was acting like some wanton slag flittered through my mind, but the moment Silver's hands ran down my body to cup my arse, I was completely lost.

Silver lifted me up and turned us around, placing me atop the counter he'd just been leaning against.

I wrapped my feet around his hips and snaked my arms up to wrap around his neck. I let him take the kiss deeper, opening my lips to his searching tongue.

Silver pushed his hips forward, pressing our groins together.

He was hard too.

I could feel it through both of our jeans.

Feeling how hard Silver was for *me* drove me wild.

I wanted, I *needed*, to feel him closer.

I tugged at his shirt, and he willingly pulled it up and off in one smooth move. I didn't get a chance to look at the splendid chest I was sure had been exposed, though, before his lips were back on mine.

His hands slipped under my shirt, his fingers stroking over my bare skin.

I arched my back, my skin tingling wherever he touched me.

Silver kissed me passionately for several more seconds, then he eventually drew back to pull my shirt off.

I lifted my arms up so he could be rid of it altogether.

His eyes took in my naked chest, and I could see on his face that he liked what he saw.

I grinned to myself and finally let my own gaze roam his chest. It was flat and toned and hairless.

He had a tattoo across his collarbone. Following the curve of it in fancy lettering were the words *memento mori*. The phrase sounded familiar, but I couldn't pinpoint exactly why. I knew I'd heard it before, but I couldn't for the life of me remember what it meant.

Both his arms were tattooed, too: a scattering of designs and colours that I couldn't make out in my lusty haze.

Silver bent back in, lips going for my neck.

I moaned and tilted my head to the side, giving him better space to nip at my skin.

He moved slowly downward, over my chest, dwelling on my nipples before going further down.

I leaned back until my shoulder blades hit the wall and arched my hips.

His hands deftly undid my fly before he pulled my jeans down and off. I was wearing tight, red boxers and my hard cock strained against them. They weren't the most fashionable piece of underwear I owned—but then I hadn't expected to take my clothes off in front of anyone today, either.

He grinned as he met my eyes and he reached down, all too slowly for my taste, and hooked his fingers under the hem. He pulled my boxers down, then swiftly bent to take my cock in his mouth.

I gasped and I had to brace my hands against the counter to keep myself upright as he sucked me thoroughly. I watched Silver through half-lidded eyes, watching how his head bobbed up and down. I could already feel my orgasm rising and I was panting heavily.

No one had ever told me I was quiet during sex.

A cry escaped me as I came; it was so unexpected that I didn't even have time to warn him about it. But he didn't seem to mind, as he continued to work me, sucking me dry.

I licked my lips as my body calmed down from the high of the orgasm and I opened my eyes, which I couldn't remember having closed in the first place.

"You're good at that." My voice was low and thick.

He licked at his own lips as he stood, plastering himself to me.

I was completely naked, except for my boxers, which had been pulled down to just under my balls. Silver kissed me and I tasted myself on his tongue.

He did swallow.

The thought seemed to sizzle through my body, starting a new fire now that the previous one had been doused.

Silver broke the kiss and smiled crookedly. "You have a nice cock."

That reminded me it was time for me to do something about his, which was poking me through the thick denim of his jeans. "My turn, then." I slid down from the counter with a grin.

Silver strode over to the black leather chair and sat down. He spread his thighs invitingly and I wasted no time falling to my knees in between them.

TT KOVE

I unzipped Silver's jeans and ran my hand over the hardness that was revealed when I pushed the flaps aside. His cock was still covered by the fabric of his boxers, so I reached inside to wrap my hand around the length. I pulled the hem down, so the erect cock came into view and I felt like drooling as I caught sight of it. It stood at proud attention, thick and hard and long.

I enveloped the head in my mouth and sucked on it, running the tip of my tongue just under the head. When I'd teased enough, until a few drops of pre-come dripped onto my tongue, I relaxed my jaw and took the length in.

I liked sucking cock; I always had, and I was good at it, too. I still hadn't forgotten my old tricks after being out of the game for a couple of months, and I put my mouth to good use now.

One of Silver's hands tangled in my hair, pulling slightly, but not so much it hurt. I rather liked the grip and the light tug.

I relaxed my jaw and took him further down my throat. Silver groaned, his hips bucking the slightest bit. I looked up at him and saw that he had his head tilted back and his eyes closed. I wanted to grin, but my mouth was full of his thick cock, which I didn't mind at all.

When he came, I swallowed it all down, just as Silver had done with me.

Silver cupped my chin in his hand and tugged me up into a kiss. I wrapped my arms around his neck as I sprawled atop him in the chair.

"Come home with me, Kian."

I smiled against his lips and tangled one hand in his black faux-hawk. "Yeah." I had work tomorrow, but if I got up a little earlier than usual, I could run home to shower and change and still be on time.

Silver kissed me again, deep and hungry, and my body responded instantly, becoming hot and hard. "Let's go *now*."

I loved the kiss, but I needed so much *more*.

Silver surged up out of the chair, all but put me down on my feet on the floor, then he continued to pull up his clothes and fasten them.

I instantly scrambled for my own.

"WE'VE GOT TO BE QUIET." He all but shoved me through the door and into the dark flat. "I've got flatmates."

"More than one?" I had a flatmate myself, so it wasn't anything new to me.

"Technically, I only have one, but my best mate's got himself a boyfriend." Silver closed the door behind us, and then guided me further into the dark flat.

His bedroom was even darker than the flat itself, mostly because the curtains were closed.

But I didn't need to see; I only needed to feel the bloke who was now pressing up against me.

I shucked my clothes in an instant, which earned me a low chuckle from him. "You, too." I laughed quietly as I turned to feel my way to the bed. I heard Silver rustle with his clothes behind me. He better be doing as I said.

When my knees hit against the side of the bed, I was suddenly tackled onto it from behind, and Silver pressed down atop me, while his mouth kissed the nape of my neck.

I let out a small gasp and I bit my lip as his tongue came out to play over my skin. My neck tingled from his attention and I was absolutely loving it. I squirmed as much as I was able to, needing friction on my cock, which had popped right back up to attention the moment Silver's skin had rubbed up against my own.

Silver's hands ran over my arms and moved down to hold my hips in place. I groaned in displeasure... until his hard, leaking cock slid between my arse-cheeks. Screw friction on my cock

—having his dick against my arse was so much better.

I gripped the bedspread tightly at the sensation of his cock sliding over my entrance. I wanted him inside me *now*, but I knew that wasn't possible. I wasn't prepared—and neither was he.

"Fuck." He muttered it against my neck, his breath fanning over my skin and making goose bumps pop up down my spine. "You feel so good."

"Will be even better if you get inside me. Like right *now*." I needed him inside so much. It had been a while since I'd slept with a bloke, and the previous one hadn't been a wet dream like Silver was. The previous one sure hadn't wanted me as much as Silver did, either.

Silver chuckled, then lifted himself off of me to rummage in his nightstand. I missed his weight, so I lay very still, hoping he would lie back down atop me when he'd found what we needed to take things further.

I heard a cap being flipped open, then the rip of a condom packet.

I turned my head to watch, but it was too dark in the room to see much of anything. I could make out that Silver was currently on his knees besides me, but that was it.

I wanted to see him roll the condom on, but it

would have to wait till later. At least I hoped there'd be a later.

Then Silver was back atop me and his slick fingers circled my entrance.

I forgot about everything but the sensation of those fingers, of that body pressing me down on the bed.

I spread my thighs wider, allowing him to settle down in-between them.

His lubed fingers played and teased over my entrance until I thought I was going to explode, until he finally pressed one in and all was right in the world.

I gasped and gripped the bedspread tighter. I buried my face in it to stifle the sounds I knew I was making. I was vocal in bed, and usually, it was a good thing, except when there were flatmates presumably on the other side of the wall.

His fingers prepared me expertly, while Silver's lips continued to scatter small kisses over my neck and shoulder blades.

When his fingers withdrew and he lifted himself off of me again, I got my knees under me and lifted my arse up from the mattress.

Silver's hands settled on my hips and I held my breath as I felt the head of his cock nudge my opening.

He pushed inside and I let out a long, drawn-out groan as I was stretched nice and good. It'd been such a long time since I'd been this close to anyone, and though it burned when his cock pressed in, it was in a good way.

When he was buried to the hilt, Silver paused.

I pushed my torso up a little to look back at him, only to have Silver drape himself over my back and kiss my neck. I tilted my head to the side, giving him more space to the thin skin.

He took the invitation and kissed, sucked, licked his way over my neck.

I knew I would have a mark, or several, come morning, but I didn't care. Silver's lips on my skin felt too divine to care about anything else.

Then he started moving his hips and my world spun. I threw my head back, resting it against Silver's, who was still kissing over my neck as he started thrusting in earnest. I couldn't stop the loud moan that escaped me.

I brought one arm up to wrap around his neck, while I kept the other braced on the bed. One of Silver's hands was braced on the bed too, while the other slid around my torso, caressing over my nipples and down my stomach until his big hand wrapped around my aching cock.

The sound of our flesh slapping together filled my

ears, together with my own moans and his low groans. I knew I wouldn't last. I could already feel the orgasm building. He was pumping me so nicely, in time with his thrusts, and I had to bite down on my lip to keep from crying out as I came all over his hand.

Silver's thrust increased in both speed and strength, and I held onto him until he emptied himself into the condom.

When he pulled out, I collapsed in a heap on the bed, my breathing laboured.

"Mmm." He lay down halfway atop me, pressing a kiss to my shoulder. "You feel amazing."

"You too." I mastered the strength to run my hand through his dark hair. "Do you think we were loud?"

He shook his head then flipped over so that he lay on his back next to me. "Hard to say in the heat of the moment."

"Well, if we were, it's no big deal. It's just sex. Completely normal."

"Not to them." Silver put his hand on the small of my back, rubbing softly. He couldn't seem to stop touching me, and I loved the constant attention. No one had ever given me so much attention before.

"What do you mean?" I rested my cheek on my folded hands and faced him in the darkness.

"They don't have sex."

"Are you taking the piss?" A startled chuckle forced its way out of me.

"Not at all." I could hear more than see him shake his head.

"Who doesn't have sex?" I was incredulous. Sure, I might've been abstinent for a couple of months, but I was no innocent virgin. Hadn't been for quite a few years. "Everybody has sex."

Silver chuckled. "Not them."

"It's impossible!" I couldn't believe what I was hearing. "How is that *possible*?"

"As long as they're happy." He pulled me to him, kissed me, then rolled us over to cover my body with his own. "So—how about round number two?"

I grinned and kissed him hard as I wrapped my legs around his middle. Oh, yeah, I was ready.

CHAPTER 3

$\mathcal{I}$ woke to a blaring alarm.

I wanted to reach out and shut it off, but I found myself to be pressed down on the bed by a warm, heavy body.

Bringing my arm out from under the pillow, I reached back to stroke it through Silver's hair. His head rested between my shoulder blades, his slow, even breathing fanning over my naked skin.

A contented sigh escaped me.

It felt *nice* waking up with him sprawled atop me.

The only thing ruining it was the blaring alarm of my phone, which I'd barely remembered to set before I'd fallen asleep.

Silver moved against me, slowly waking up. He rolled away, breaking the contact I'd liked so much.

With a sigh, I bent over to the nightstand and switched the alarm off.

I lay back down and rested my cheek on my folded hands. I didn't want to get up. It felt good lying in bed with Silver at my side. I didn't want it to end.

He rolled back over to my side. One of his hands slid over my back and he rested his chin on my shoulder. "Last night was really great." His voice was sleep-roughened, but the complete honesty shone right through it. "I hope we can do it again?"

A warm feeling spread in the pit of my stomach. "Yeah, we can definitely do this again." I turned my face to bury it in my hands, hiding the ridiculous smile I knew was on my face.

Silver was silent for a while, but he kept his chin perched on my shoulder.

It tickled a little, in an entirely good way.

"Would you mind it terribly if I asked you out to lunch today?"

"I wouldn't mind at all." That warm, happy feeling spread through my body, until it felt like I was tingling all over. "How about at one?"

"That works." His arm squeezed me tight and I realised in that moment that he'd been nervous about my answer.

As if he's got anything to worry about.

He was a walking wet dream come true and seemingly with a personality to match. I wasn't going to let him go. Not without a heck of a fight.

My phone started blaring again and I huffed as I leaned over to shut it off for good. "I really have to go." I didn't want to, and for a moment I contemplated calling in sick, but he had his own job to get to in a little while, so there was no point to it.

Besides, I would see him again in just a few hours. For lunch. That could be classified as a date, couldn't it? I didn't have much experience—more like none—with dating, but I was pretty sure that would be changing today.

"All right." Silver seemed reluctant to let me go, but in the end, he pulled his arm back and flopped over so that he was lying on his back.

I leaned over and kissed his cheek.

"Thanks for an amazing night, Silver."

I started searching for my clothes, which had ended up in a heap a bit away, right where I'd stripped down the night before.

Silver watched me as I got dressed and it sent good, tingling goose bumps down my spine. To think that this gorgeous bloke found *me* gorgeous! It was quite unbelievable.

"See you at one." I grinned down at him as I pulled on my jumper.

"I'll stop by the salon." He grinned back and my heart skipped a beat.

I'm already beginning to fall for him.

I had never thought I was one of those people who fell so easily for someone else, but I was officially proven quite the opposite.

With one last smile, I exited Silver's room.

I closed the door carefully behind me, then turned around to find myself face-to-face with a black-haired, blue-eyed bloke who looked maybe more shocked than me at meeting someone this early in the morning.

In his own flat, nonetheless.

But then I knew Silver had flatmates.

And this one must not have known that Silver had had an overnight visitor, judging from the surprised look.

I guess we were quiet after all, then.

"Hey," I said, from lack of anything better to say.

I got a mumbled greeting in return and a once-over.

"Sorry, I got to dash." I inched around him, feeling misplaced and awkward around Silver's flatmate when I hadn't even met the bloke before. Something teased at my memory about him, but I couldn't grab at it and it slipped away as I stepped into my Converse and left the flat.

~

CHLOE GRINNED at me when I hurried into work with five minutes to spare.

"How was your night?"

"You totally set me up!" I wheezed at her. "You are so amazing!" I hugged her tight for a brief moment before shedding my jacket and hanging it up on the coat hanger.

"I knew you'd like him." She leaned against the wall next to me with her arms crossed over her chest. "Silver's a walking wet dream."

"Mmhmm." *My thoughts exactly.* I couldn't agree more. I was even so lucky as to have seen him *naked.*

"So—?" She stuck her head forward in a curious motion.

I blinked at her as I hung up my bag. "So what?"

"So what happens now? Between you two? It wasn't just a one-off, was it?"

"He asked me to lunch today." I couldn't stop the wide smile that erupted.

To think that Silver had asked *me* to lunch.

That he seemed to want more than just a one night stand.

I still couldn't fathom it.

These things didn't happen to me.

Chloe smiled too. "I'm so happy for you." She playfully ruffled my hair.

"Hey!" I tried to fend her off. "Don't touch the hair!" I lifted both my hands up to do damage control, then gave her a narrowed look.

She only laughed at me and flounced off back into the salon.

Once my hair was back in perfect order, I followed her.

I had work to do—and then I had a date to attend. I was sure the morning would drag on, now that I had something to look forward to, but not even that could douse my happiness.

Several of my regulars were in today, and they all commented that I seemed particularly happy.

I found it baffling, because really, did it show that much? I was always happy and smiling and chitchatting. I didn't think anyone would perceive me as being *happier*. I was perfectly happy every minute I was at work. How could I not be when I was doing what I loved?

Silver showed up right on time. I was finishing up cleaning my station when I spotted him, and my heart instantly sped up. I hurried into the back room to get my bag and my jacket. I didn't want to keep him waiting.

He smiled when I approached and my stomach flipped over in answer.

Blimey, he makes me so nervous.

"People have been commenting on my good mood all day," I said by way of greeting. "It's all your fault."

He laughed, and then slid his hand over my back to lightly rest it on my opposite shoulder.

I shivered at the contact and stepped closer.

"Ready for lunch?"

"You bet." I was ready for more, *so much more*, but it was the middle of the day, so lunch was likely all I was going to get.

Silver kept his arm around me as we exited the salon. I really liked the feel of it there.

We ended up at Subway, as it was the closest and we both only had half an hour lunch break.

Silver ordered an Oven-Roasted Chicken sub, while I chose the Veggie Delight salad. He paid for us both, even though I tried to object. It was a sweet gesture, though, so when he insisted, I let him do whatever he wanted.

"So you're a vegetarian?" He eyed my salad once we'd found an available table for two.

"More like a semi-vegetarian."

He grinned. "That doesn't really tell me much."

"Well, I eat dairy products, eggs, chicken and fish,

but I stay away from any other meat." I stabbed my fork through a piece of salad. "Besides, salads and vegetables are yummy."

"That's true, though I do like a good steak with it." Silver took a bite of his chicken sub after throwing me a wry grin.

I smiled back.

He wasn't just good in bed; he was also good at making me feel comfortable. I couldn't deny I was nervous, I'd never done anything like this before, after all, but sitting here now with him was nice. Having lunch with him, talking with him... I liked it a lot.

I didn't want lunch to end.

"So I wanted to ask you..."

Oh no, here it comes.

I put my fork down and looked resolutely at the table top. Maybe Silver hadn't enjoyed what we'd shared as much as I had and now I got the rejection. I didn't want to be rejected, not by this wonderful bloke who had seemed to really like me—

"... if you would like to go on a proper date with me?"

"Huh?" I lifted my head and blinked at him in confusion. "You want to date me? For real?"

A warm smile spread on his oh-so-kissable lips. "Of course I do. Why else would I have gone to all the trouble just to meet you? I had to bribe Chloe into bringing you with her just to get you to notice me. I can't believe how *you* could say yes."

"Are you taking the piss?" I stared at him, wide-eyed. "You are the most gorgeous bloke I've ever seen! Not to say that this is like only skin-deep or anything, but you are bloody gorgeous. And to top it off, you seem to have a really nice personality, too. I can be so daft at times. I can't believe I never noticed you. I really just want to smack myself in the face."

He chuckled. "Well, don't do *that*. Wouldn't want to hurt that pretty face." His gaze was intense as he looked at me.

I could feel the blush creep up into my cheeks.

"So is that a yes?"

I blinked again, unable to look away from those grey eyes.

"Do you want to date me, Kian?"

"I thought I already made that clear?" It felt like my wide smile was glued to my face. I couldn't stop smiling for the life of me. "Yes, I want to date you, Silver."

His smile was brilliant, happy, and I couldn't help myself.

I bent over the table to kiss him.

I had no idea what exactly it was he saw in me, but that happiness couldn't be faked.

"Do you want to come over tonight? We could have dinner together. You could meet my flatmates."

That sounded like a brilliant idea, but... "I promised my dad that I'd come have dinner with them tonight. But I can come over afterwards? I'd love to spend the evening with you *and* meet your flatmates."

His hand gripped the side of my head, holding me there bent over the table, so he could kiss me. "That sounds great. You know where I live, just come over whenever you're free. I'll be home."

The giddiness I felt right then couldn't even be described.

I might miss out on dinner with him today, but we were dating now, and that would certainly mean other dinners in the future.

I couldn't wait.

CHAPTER 4

"***Y***ou seem happy."

"Hmm?" I glanced at Sun-Hi, my step-mum, as I decked the table for four.

"You. Seem. Happy." She pointed a finger at me to emphasise her words from where she was standing in front of the cooker.

Did everyone notice that today?

I didn't think I looked any different than usual, but something must be different, since everyone kept commenting on it. "Well, I think I might've just got myself a boyfriend."

"You think?" She frowned, confused.

"Well, yeah. We're dating. I guess that's the same?

I've never had a boyfriend before. Or dated anyone, for that matter."

She blinked—and I realised exactly what kind of information I was sharing with my step-mum. She knew I hadn't been celibate prior to getting to know her, or after, and I'd done a lot of things I wasn't exactly proud of.

"Are we going to meet this lucky bloke?"

"Uh, well." No. Maybe eventually, but… "It just happened. Like, I literally only met him yesterday. I need to get to know him a bit better before I introduce him to my family, you know."

"Of course." She smiled. "Whenever you're ready."

I returned the smile, grateful that she even wanted to meet whoever I was dating. If I'd still been in contact with my mum, it wouldn't have been the case. She'd never given a shit. But my dad and his family, they did.

They'd welcomed me with open arms without even knowing me properly.

"So how's Chloe?" Dad asked when we were seated at the table.

"Oh, you know." I waved my hand as if waving the subject away. "She's busy with work and her girl-friend, but we manage to squeeze in some quality time together now and then."

Dad smiled, but his gaze was steady on me. "You know you can move back in here anytime, right?"

"I'm doing fine, Dad." I returned the smile. "I want to make my own living. Have my own space. And Chloe and I, we're great flatmates."

Besides, moving back in would mean sharing a room with a ten-year old. I loved my little brother, I really did, but sharing a room when I was eighteen wasn't exactly something I wished for. They didn't have a lot of money, so their flat wasn't that big. Before I'd finished my A-levels, I'd stayed out many nights—hence why they *all* knew I hadn't ever been celibate.

"Besides, it's close to work and close to city central." I loved living close to everything that happened.

I wouldn't have to worry about train times to get back home. I could catch the bus, the tube, or just walk if I wasn't too far away.

And Chloe had turned into more than just my flatmate since we met through work—she was my best friend.

"You know the offer always stands." Dad started cutting up Kasey's chicken, while Sun-Hi piled food on her own plate.

I smiled at my little brother, who grinned back. He was missing two canine teeth in the front, one on both sides, and the gap only made him look more adorable. Kasey was sweet, shy, and just an all-around nice kid.

I'd never had a brother before, but it was all good.

Kasey wasn't an annoyance—in fact, I'd never seen a ten year old be as *good* as Kasey was. But sharing a room with him wasn't ideal. Though, that was more me, my hormones, and my need for personal space than him.

"Kian just started dating someone." Sun-Hi said it lightly, as if it wasn't a majorly important piece of information.

Maybe it wasn't to them, maybe it was just me.

Still, it was interesting enough for her to bring it up at dinner.

"Oh?" Dad's eyebrows rose as he focused on me again. "What's he like?"

If Dad had been the kind of person not to accept me for who I was back on that day, I wouldn't have wanted anything to do with him. Thankfully, he had been very accepting, even when faced with the first time I'd spent the night away. He hadn't blinked an eye when I came home still dressed in the clothes from the previous day and dishevelled.

"He's fantastic." I knew I was grinning goofily now, but I couldn't help myself. "He's real good-looking and to top it off, his personality's great too."

"I asked if we could meet him, but Kian's being possessive of him." Sun-Hi didn't look at me, too busy cutting up her own chicken, but I heard the teasing tone.

"Oh, come on! I just met the poor bloke. Can't throw him to the family just yet."

"When are you meeting him again?" Dad smiled at his wife's antics, but he turned his serious question to me.

"Today. After dinner."

In fact, as much as I loved having dinner with them, I couldn't wait for it to end.

I STOOD in front of his door, all nervous now about the impending meeting with not just Silver, but with his flatmates as well.

What if they didn't like me?

I wasn't an easy person to like.

A lot of people judged me solely from the way I dressed or acted. But then again, his flatmates were gay, so surely they would be more open-minded?

I knocked tentatively.

There were a few moments of me moving uncomfortably, then I froze up completely as the door opened.

"Hey, you." Silver smiled widely at me.

What had I even been afraid of?

Warmth spread through my chest, and I grinned stupidly back. "Hey."

"Come on in, Kian." He got out of the way so I could brush past him. While I stepped out of my shoes, he closed the door.

I straightened up, and let my gaze take him in from bottom to top while I did. He wore much the same as yesterday: jeans and a tight tee, only in a different colour. I almost drooled at the thought of being able to worship that broad chest—especially as I still hadn't even had a proper look at it.

Silver led me over to the sofa.

I looked around, but we were the only ones there. I wondered where his flatmates were, seeing as I was supposed to meet them.

"I'm glad you came." He sat down right next to me. Our thighs and shoulders pressed together.

I didn't mind at all. I rather liked feeling him besides me.

"I'm glad you asked me, even if I had plans earlier."

He leaned in close to me. "So, we weren't that quiet last night after all." He kissed me, but it was just a chaste lips-on-lips kiss.

"They heard us?"

"Josh did. But only because he went to the bathroom last night. He doesn't mind, though. It would've been worse if Damian heard." He chuckled.

"He's the one who doesn't like se—" I broke off as I caught sight of a door opening, and the black-haired lad from that morning came walking out with a blond bloke at his heels.

"Hey." Silver turned his attention to them as they came over the other sofa. "This is Kian." He nodded to me. "And this is Damian," the black-haired one, "and Josh," the blond.

"Hey." I did a small wave, unsure of what to say or what to do in this kind of situation. I'd never been in it before and it was *daunting*.

They both greeted me in return, the blond one sounding a lot nicer than the dark one. My eyes were still drawn to him though, because the feeling from that morning just intensified.

Damian.

"You're Chloe's… something."

Blue eyes came to rest on me. "She's my aunt's sister, yeah."

I snapped my fingers. "I knew it. I knew there was something familiar about you when I met you this morning. I just couldn't pinpoint it, because we haven't ever actually *met*."

His eyes narrowed a fraction. "Then how do you know who I am?"

"I've seen a couple of pictures of you." And Chloe did mention him from time to time. They weren't close, but she did have pictures of him and the rest of her family, pinned to her bedroom wall.

He only nodded and leaned back.

I couldn't read him, or how he felt about me recognising him from Chloe's pictures.

The blond—Josh?—curled up on the other side of him, knees tucked up and his arms wrapped around them. He seemed kind of sad.

"You've had dinner?" I asked Silver. It was the first topic I could think of.

"Yeah." He slid his arm over my back, caressing me softly.

I shuddered.

It was a good kind of shudder, the one that desperately wanted more.

"How was dinner with your family?"

"Nice. Like it always is. I was a bit anxious to be done, though."

His grin told me he got the subtext.

Anxious to see him.

I'm glad he got it.

I might've only met him yesterday, but I definitely had feelings. Not as much as he, as he'd apparently had his eyes on me long before last night, but I was sure they'd get there.

We spent some time on the sofa, watching the telly. They didn't speak much, and I had no idea what to say.

I didn't know any of them.

"Stay over tonight?" Silver whispered the question into my ear. His arm had been resting along the back of the sofa, but now it slipped down to settle over my shoulder.

Once again, I shuddered, both from the weight of his arm and from his question. I knew what that would lead to, and I looked forward to it.

I nodded quickly. "I have to get up just as early tomorrow too, though. Work and all that."

"That's okay." He nipped at my earlobe and I sucked in a breath. I got all hot and bothered, and my tight jeans just became a bit tighter in a certain area.

He must've noticed it.

Or maybe he had the same problem, because he asked, "Bed now?"

"Yes!"

He held onto my hand as we made our way around the sofa that his flatmates were still sitting in, and across the floor until we reached his bedroom door.

Once we were inside and the door was closed, he pushed me up against it and kissed me.

Lust coursed through my body and I tangled my fingers in his hair, holding him right there against me. His body was big: wider and more muscular than mine, and it was *hot*. The way he covered me, all of me, was too hot for words to describe.

His hands grubbed my arse-cheeks, pulled me in further against him and up so our groins rubbed together. I wrapped my legs around his thighs so as to easily hold myself *right* there.

"Fuck, you feel so good." He grabbed me tighter, then turned us both around and made his way over to the bed.

In one smooth motion, I was on my back and he bore down atop me.

The lust made me hazy, and I fumbled my hands down to his zipper. The clothes definitely needed to go.

He pulled back to be rid of them completely, then helped me shimmy out of mine. He stretched back out atop me once we were both naked and all felt right in my world.

It shouldn't be this all-consuming on the second day I'd known him, and the second time we had sex, but it was.

It was good and scary and everything in between.

And I really hoped this would be more than just hooking up, more than just dating, that we would be real boyfriends and be together.

I'd never had that before—but I wanted it with him.

That I knew already.

CHAPTER 5

"*I* didn't really get a feel of your flatmates."

My head rested on his chest and my index finger circled his nipple.

"They didn't say much."

His right hand carded through my hair, while the left rested on his stomach. "Josh's had a bad day. They're not usually *that* closed off."

Well, everyone was entitled to having a bad day.

I couldn't judge that.

I had a lot of bad days myself. Though maybe not as much lately.

"So you know Chloe through Damian?" I asked him.

"Yeah. I met Damian beginning of the last year in college."

Quick math told me what I needed to know. "So you're as old as we are then."

"Actually, no."

I lifted my head slightly to look at him, blinking in surprise. "You were done with college when you met Damian?" Damian was as old as Chloe and I, all of us were eighteen. If Silver wasn't our year, how old was he?

Was he *younger*?

Had I just shagged a seventeen-year-old?

"I had to retake the last year. I'm nineteen." It sounded final, like he didn't want to elaborate on the reason he'd had to retake the year.

I could respect that.

We'd only known each other two days after all, so I couldn't expect to get his life story just yet.

"An older man, huh?" I grinned, then put my head back down on his chest. I moved my hand down to squeeze his.

He tangled our fingers together and I smiled against his skin.

"Not that much older." His fingers tightened in my hair, playfully pulling just the tiniest bit.

"How long have your flatmates been together?"

"A week."

That brought me up short. "Only a week?" Like I'd told him, I hadn't got a good feel of them earlier, so I hadn't been able to judge just how comfortable they were with each other.

But just a week… that was surprising.

I'd expected a longer time-frame.

"They clicked. They met and that was it."

"They didn't know each other from before?"

"No. They literally just met a week ago."

And we'd literally met two days ago.

His chest moved under me as he chuckled.

"I joked with Damian the other day about how he could get a boyfriend before I did. He's not the easiest person to get close to, after all. But then, it didn't take me long after to get one of my own."

My heart jumped at the mention of the B-word. I gripped his hand tighter, my stomach fluttering with butterflies.

Boyfriends.

I liked that word.

It was the most beautiful word in the *world*.

His thumb stroked over the back of my hand as he resumed stroking my hair with the other.

It was all so nice and relaxing.

"What's your favourite colour?"

Huh?

I scrunched my nose up in thought. "I don't think

I really have one. It all depends. Used to be green, thus why I had green hair. Now I'm kinda in between."

"That's why you have rainbow-dyed tips?"

"Yeah, I guess." Whenever I got hooked on a new colour I thought would look good, I dyed my hair. I was pretty happy with the black with rainbow tips at the moment, but I knew myself well enough to know it wouldn't last for long. I didn't have the best attention span, so I would soon be bored with my current colour. "Why are you asking about that?" I turned my head slightly so I could look up at him.

"Just trying to get to know you."

"So we're having a round of twenty questions?"

"It *is* effective."

"Okay then." I kissed his skin lightly. "What's *your* favourite colour?"

"Green."

"That's why I caught your attention? Because my hair was green?"

"It was after that I found I quite liked green." He lifted his head off the pillow so he could look down at me too. "And your eyes... they're green, too. I like it."

I stared into his eyes.

I quite liked the grey colour of them, but saying

so now, when he'd just complemented the colour of mine, would be a bit stupid.

Wouldn't it?

I had no idea how these kinds of things worked. I'd never had anyone give me such compliments before. The other blokes I'd been with had mostly complimented me on my ability to suck cock.

"Have you always known you wanted to be a hairdresser?"

So apparently we *were* doing twenty questions.

"Yeah, pretty much. I've always liked hair. Cutting it, styling it, colouring it. I like to make people feel pretty." The only thing I'd had when I grew up were my looks. I hadn't had the prettiest clothes, because my mother couldn't ever bother to spend money on me when she could use it on herself, but at least I'd been able to keep my hair the way I wanted and put make-up on my face.

Not that I used much—but eyeliner was a must.

I pushed the thoughts away to focus on him. It was so much better to stay in the present than dwell on the past, especially when it was as depressing as mine. "Have you always known you wanted to be a tattoo artist?"

"I've always been good at art. I knew I had to do something like that when I finished school. Back when I had my first tattoo done, I was sold. I had to do it. I had to get an apprenticeship. And I did, when I got here, after I finished the last year of college."

Got here?

"You're not from London?" I couldn't place his dialect; it wasn't that distinct from mine. If he hadn't mentioned it, I would've just assumed he was born and bred in the city, just like I was.

"Ah, no. I moved here after—well, I retook the last year of A-levels here. I moved in with my brother."

"What about your parents?" He'd had to retake a year for a reason. Surely he hadn't lost them?

"They're still living in the house my brother and I grew up in. They're... older, though. They hadn't planned on having a second child, so Vincent's eleven years older than me. I was the accident that wasn't supposed to happen, but they're religious, too, so being rid of me was out of the question."

He talked about them in a detached kind of way. "You're not close with your parents?"

"Not really. They're older; they don't understand why I do what I do and why I want to look like I do. They love me, I know they do, but it's difficult when they can't understand. I'm the odd one, while Vincent's always been the normal one." He didn't sound particularly sad about it, but then, he might be hiding it.

"If it makes you feel any better, I'm not even in contact with my mother." I was definitely not sad about that fact.

"How come?" He peered curiously at me.

"She's a bitch. She only kept me around out of spite to my dad, who she managed to keep away for my entire childhood."

His eyebrows rose. "That's messed up. Where's your dad now?"

"Here in London. He contacted me the day I turned eighteen, and told me the truth. We've got a good relationship now, even if I've only known them five months."

"Them?"

"My dad, stepmother, and little brother."

I could tell he was surprised. "You didn't know any of them until five months ago?"

I shook my head. "No. My mother won sole custody when dad left her, years ago, and she refused to let him see me ever since. Out of spite, as I said, because she couldn't handle him leaving her, you know."

"Damn, Ki. That—sucks." He grimaced slightly.

"Everyone's got family issues. I've yet to meet someone who hasn't."

"Well, that's true. To some degree, anyway."

I put my head back down on his chest again. It

was smooth—likely shaved, but I wasn't about to complain. I didn't have body hair myself: didn't like it at all.

I didn't mind it on others, as long as it wasn't excessively much, but there was nothing quite as drool-worthy as a broad, toned, smooth-shaven chest. I could just lick him all day long, if possible.

"So, how'd you meet Damian?"

"Quite randomly, to be honest. A few days into the term, I saw him sitting alone at a table, so I asked if I could sit with him. We just continued sitting together at lunch after that, and now we're best friends and flatmates. It's wonderful, really, he's a good mate."

"I've only got Chloe as a mate. We met at work, but we started spending time together outside of it, too, and then we decided to get a flat together. It's nice when you meet a person you just click with like that, in that you instantly know that you're going to be great friends."

I'd never been spoiled with friends either, but once Chloe and I met, I hadn't minded it so much.

Now that I'd met Silver, I didn't mind it at all.

It probably wasn't the healthiest train of thoughts, but I wanted to spend every single spare second I had with him. As long as it lasted, anyhow.

Please let it last a long time.

I lowered my gaze, and caught sight of the duvet over his hips. It was raised over his crotch and I couldn't help but grin.

I extricated my hand from his and slipped it under the duvet.

He drew in a sharp breath once my hand made contact. "You want to go another round?"

"You want to talk more?"

"Well, yeah." But he spread his thighs apart, giving me more room to stroke his cock. "I do want to get to know you properly."

"Hmm." I thought over the topics we'd covered. "Have you been in a relationship before?" I wasn't sure if that was something you were supposed to ask about or not, but what the hell. I was curious.

"Yeah. One. You?" That was another admission from him that came out quickly, and which sounded final, like he didn't want to elaborate further.

Curiosity burned in me, but we were new. If there was something, I hoped he'd tell me when he trusted me more.

As for now… two days weren't enough for that.

"Nope. Never had a boyfriend."

"How's that even possible?"

"What'd you mean?"

"You're gorgeous. How can you not have had blokes throwing themselves at your feet?"

A laugh escaped me. "Are you taking the piss?" I pushed myself up on my elbows so I could look him properly in the eyes. They were sincere, and my laughter died. "You're *not* taking the piss?"

"Why would I be?" His eyes searched mine.

"I've never been popular. People think I'm too much."

"I like too much." He grinned. "But, truthfully, Kian, I think you're beautiful."

"You're the one with the good looks around here." I couldn't help but point it out. When I wore make-up, I reckoned I was good-looking, but without... I looked pretty ordinary.

He, on the other hand, couldn't look ordinary if he tried.

He pushed himself up on his elbows, too, until his lips brushed mine. "Maybe we can agree to disagree."

I couldn't think when his lips were so close.

Nor with his cock all hard and leaking pre-come in my hand.

"Sounds like a good idea." I tilted my chin just the tiniest bit up, and that was all it took for our lips to meet properly.

His tongue ran over my bottom lip and I parted them, letting him inside. He took full advantage and

I couldn't have stopped the moan that escaped me even if I'd wanted to.

"I'll suck you off," I offered in a murmur once our lips only hovered close again.

"I won't say no to that." He nipped at my lip. "I'll suck you off afterwards. Or we could suck *each other* off."

I shivered at the mere mention of it. "Yes, let's."

And so all thoughts of getting to know one another better, of asking simple questions, were blown away.

Quite literally.

CHAPTER 6

*J*jostled awake by Silver jerking, but before I could roll over to ask if everything was okay, he was out of the bed and tip-toeing out of the room.

I blinked myself further into awareness. The way he'd jerked awake, it was like he'd had a nightmare.

I wasn't sure if I should get up and look for him or if he needed to be alone.

I heard something then. Muffled voices and someone hurrying into the bathroom, which was right next to the wall I was lying against.

What the hell's going on?

It wasn't just Silver in there, which meant one or both of his flatmates had to be as well. Now I definitely should just stay in bed. What could they be doing up and about in the middle of the night, anyway?

I thought I heard sobbing as well as the muffled voices.

Someone's upset.

I bit my lip. Both curious and worried about what could've possibly happened to cause those kinds of sobs.

But I should remain where I was. I was a newcomer, and I didn't know his flatmates. It'd been two days since I officially met them, and I hadn't spoken many words with either of them since.

I rolled onto my back to stare up at the ceiling. When I faced the wall, it felt like I was eavesdropping, even though I couldn't actually hear what they were saying in there.

Muffled voices still came through to me.

I reached over to flick on the lamp on the bedside table, then checked my mobile for the time.

2:49. Middle of the night, all right.

I had work in the morning, which meant I should go back to sleep, but I couldn't now. Not when worrying. What if it was Silver who was upset?

I didn't know how long I lay there, staring at nothing in particular, but the door eventually inched open.

I sat up and wrapped my arms around my knees as I watched him.

As soon as he realised the light was on, his eyes were on me. He smiled sadly as he closed the door behind him, but his eyes were dry and there were no evidence of tears. Which meant it was one of his flat-mates who had been crying.

"Everything all right?"

He didn't speak as he crossed the floor, and he sighed heavily once he dropped down on the bed. "Did you hear much of it? I know the walls aren't very thick."

"No, not really. All I heard was muffled voices and sobbing. What's wrong?"

Silver bowed his head to look at his hands. "Josh is having a hard time."

"Is he going to be all right?" Even if I didn't know him, I still cared. He obviously meant a lot to Silver, even if he'd only known him for a week longer than I had.

"Who knows?" He shook his head. He glanced sideways at me, teeth out to bite down on his lip. "I'm not sure it's a secret or anything, but you're with me now, so I think you need to know some things."

I frowned. "What things?"

"Josh has a mental illness. It's, apparently, both a mental illness *and* brain-damage. It's called borderline personality disorder. Basically, it's a lack of control of emotions, at least from what I've gathered so far. But Josh also self-harms."

I had never heard of that particular mental illness.

But brain-damage… that sounded very, very serious.

As did self-injuring.

"What does he do?"

"Cuts his arms. He's got a horrible past, Kian, and I don't even know a quarter of it. But what I've heard so far is horrible enough. No one should have to deal with what he's had to deal with." His gaze fastened somewhere to my side, but his eyes seemed far away, like he was in deep thoughts.

I didn't know what to say.

My past wasn't that good, I didn't think, but it wasn't horrible either. It could've been a lot worse than just being neglected by my own mother.

From the sound of it, Josh'd had more than that happen to him. It truly was horrible.

"Why were you up in the first place?" I reached over to stroke a hand over his shoulder.

He snapped out of his thoughts. "I had a bad dream. I didn't want to wake you, so I left the room."

I refrained from telling him he had woken me up.

He rubbed a finger over his temple. "Josh was

curled up on the bathroom floor. I went to get Damian and then we cleaned him up."

I gripped his shoulder tight for a moment. "You're a good mate, Silver."

He smiled slightly. "I like to think so. Josh means a lot to Damian—and I've come to care for him, too. He's real sweet, but also real broken."

I scooted over to sit close to him. My hand slipped down his back to grip his waist, and my cheek rested against his shoulder. "He's lucky to have you both."

Another slight smile. "Damian tries his best. I do too, whenever I can help. I've never seen him take an interest in anyone, so it's quite nice that he finally does."

"There's never been anything between the two of you?" I asked teasingly.

He barked a laugh. "No. If such were the case, it would've been disastrous." He turned to me, his smile wide and sincere now. "A complete and utter tragedy."

"How come?"

"Damian is possibly the most private person I have ever known. And he doesn't like sex, has no interest in it whatsoever, whereas I *love* it."

I remembered him saying something about sex

the first night we'd hooked up. "How can they be in a relationship and not have sex? Are they waiting?"

He shook his head slowly, grin turning amused. "He doesn't want it. And Josh... I don't know. Pretty sure he's been through enough."

"I can't help it, but I think it's weird that someone doesn't like sex. I mean, they should at least *try* it, see the awesomeness they're missing out on."

He laughed again, then pulled me down with him on the bed. "I'm glad I've found someone who likes it just as much as I do."

"Oh, you bet." Now that I was with him, I couldn't even imagine ever going without sex. It wasn't so bad when I'd been free and single—but just being in Silver's presence made me hot for him.

"YOU LOOK AMAZING."

Silver's arms slid around my shoulders, and he bent down to kiss my neck softly.

I tilted my head to the side, giving him better space, hoping he'd take the hint and just keep on kissing me. "So do you."

We were both in club gear. Skin-tight black jeans and a tight tee, with a waistcoat over it, for me. My hair was styled just so, with a bit of glitter in it, and my make-up was even more dramatic than usual.

I looked quite good, if I had to say so myself.

And he... well, he was good enough to drool over, as usual.

He wore black trousers with a belt and a tight vest that perfectly showed off his muscular, tattooed arms. His hair was styled up at the top and ruffled in the back, with his sides styled forward.

"Maybe we should ask Josh to come out with us?" I still hadn't been able to get to know either him nor Damian much. I hadn't seen much of them this past week, after Josh's breakdown in the bathroom.

Silver's kisses on my neck stopped. I turned my head to look at him, and he seemed thoughtful. "Guess I could ask."

"Maybe it'll be good for him? Get out and get something else to think about?" Damian was working the late shift, so Josh was alone. "And it's an opportunity for me to get to know him better."

"That it is." Silver ran his hand over my cheek. "I'll go ask him."

He exited the bathroom, and I turned back to the mirror. I smoothed out my waistcoat, applied cologne, and then I was ready to pull.

Except I already had pulled—and would be going back with him tonight.

"Josh is in." Silver met me in the living room, arms wrapping around my waist and twirling me around against him. "He seemed excited about it, too. Good thing you mentioned it to me. Damian doesn't like to go clubbing, so I didn't even think about asking Josh."

I stood up on my tip-toes so I could lean in for a kiss.

He answered it enthusiastically, and we kept right on kissing until Josh finished up in the bathroom.

"You're looking good!" I winked at him after taking him in. Jeans and a shirt weren't anything I would ever wear when I went clubbing, but then, Josh wasn't anything like me. He was quite good-looking with his fair complexion, ruffled blond hair, and green eyes.

Only thing I could put my finger on was that he was too thin.

He smiled shyly at the compliment. "You look good, too. Both of you do."

"So do you." Silver reached over to clap his shoulder.

"Let's go!" I was entirely too excited about a night out. I hadn't been out clubbing in a long time, and even if I wasn't out to pull now, it would still be fun.

~

"Shots?" I yelled it into Josh's ear so he'd hear me over the loud music.

He nodded in answer, and I leaned over the counter to yell my order in the bartender's ear next.

He gestured he got me and filled the six shot glasses I'd requested.

Josh's eyes were wide when I slid three over to him.

"Shows on." I downed my shots instantly, one after the other, and I watched as he did the same. "Now that's going to get things started." I pushed the glasses further in on the counter, away from us, then turned around so I could see the dance floor.

Silver approached us. He'd been held up at the door by someone he knew when we'd arrived.

He grinned, grabbed me, and then twirled me around so that I leant back against him, while he was the one leaning against the counter.

"Smooth," I commented, then leaned in to kiss him. It wasn't easy kissing him, because one kiss always led to a second one, and a third one, and then we were necking on happily.

I pulled back because I felt bad for Josh, him being alone and all, but then I saw he was chatting with someone else, so I grinned at Silver and leaned back in for another kiss.

He was happy to oblige.

We were pressed together and I could feel him harden through his loose trousers. I did too, but my skin-tight jeans did a better job at keeping my cock firmly in place.

Eventually I had to pull back, or else I wouldn't have been able to stop myself from ripping his clothes off right there. He turned towards me, so my body shielded certain parts of him, then discreetly reached down to position himself so he was more presentable.

A laugh escaped me.

I couldn't help it.

He only grinned at me, wrapped one arm around my waist, and turned to Josh, who was now conversing with not one, but two strangers.

Silver put a hand on his shoulder, which finally brought Josh's attention back to our side. "Want another drink?"

"I'll have whatever you're having." He handed Silver some money he drew up from his pocket.

Silver turned to order, but I eyed Josh's companions curiously. "Who're your friends?"

"Oh. This is Leslie and Spencer." He motioned to each of them as he said their names.

I shook both their hands. "I'm Kian. Nice to meet you." They both greeted me back, but I did a double turn once I heard the blond named Leslie speak. "Where're you from, love?"

He smiled indulgently, like he got that question a lot. He likely did. "Newcastle."

"Proper Geordie, huh?"

He laughed good-naturedly. "Starting to turn into a proper Londoner by now."

Silver turned back around and handed Josh his drink.

Josh took a sip, grimacing slightly, before taking another one. Silver leaned in close to him and said something I didn't catch in his ear.

I looked back to Josh's mates.

"You together?" They didn't stand particularly close, but I had a feeling I was right.

The brunet nodded. I'd already forgotten his name. "We are."

"How long?"

"Almost a year now."

"Wow. I can't even imagine." I cut a wry glance at Silver, who still leant in close to Josh. Would we still be together in a year? Or would whatever was between us now have faded by then?

Silver stood back, eyes resting on Josh, who now took a big sip of his drink.

"Want to dance with me?" I fisted my hands in his vest, drawing him in closer to me. When he only grinned, I dragged him with me out on the dance floor.

I moulded myself to his body once we were out there and we moved to the thumping music. We gyrated together, hands gripping each other, lips sliding over one another.

It was perfect and I really hoped we'd be exactly like this one year from now.

CHAPTER 7

"*I* have two words for you."

I glanced at Chloe as I finished blowing all the hair off my station with the blow-dryer. "What?"

"Double date."

"Are you mental?" I put the blow-dryer back in its place and went over to get the broom.

"It's a good idea! You and Silver, me and Quinn. What's wrong with that?"

"Going on a double date with lesbians? Really?"

"You're such a racist tosser."

"Are we different races now?" I had to egg her on. It was too much fun not to.

"Oh, come on. You know what I mean. Why can't you go on a date with us?"

"Because we're two blokes and you're two gals, and then everyone's just going to assume that we're two straight couples double-dating."

She stared at me, completely unimpressed. "That makes absolutely no sense. No one's ever going to mistake you for a straight bloke. If there's anything you should worry about, it's that people will think Silver's straight when you're out with him."

My eyes narrowed. "Thanks a lot."

"You're welcome." She rolled her eyes and turned away from me, heading over to clean up her own station. "Think about it, though. It's a brilliant idea."

"Kian, there's someone here to see you!"

I swept the remaining hairs from my station before walking to the front of the salon, where my boss was standing at the register, ringing up her own customer.

I'd expected to see Silver, even if he hadn't agreed to lunch today, but there was only a bloke I'd never seen before in my life.

"Can I help you?" I stepped around the register, away from my boss and her customer, to face him. He was maybe a couple of years older than me.

"Kian, yes?" He looked at me, particularly at my hair. "Your hair... wasn't it green?"

"There's a thing called colouring." I crossed my

arms over my chest. "I'm sorry, but... do I know you? How do you know me?"

He blinked. His brown hair was shaggily unkempt, and it didn't seem like it was done on purpose, either. He was pale and his brown eyes were dull. "Ahh, we—well, we hooked up once a couple of months ago?" He made it sound like a question, like he wasn't sure of it himself. "At Heaven?"

I flashed back to an evening I'd been particularly peeved with something or another, and to top it off, I'd also been feeling rather lonely. I'd gone out to try to enjoy myself and to feel a bit better.

I remembered drinking a lot, lots of shots, and dirty dancing with someone, then I'd stumbled into the toilets with him and we'd exchanged blowjobs.

This was him?

It wasn't a very kind thought, but I must've been quite desperate that night. He wasn't my type at all. None of my previous hook-ups had anything on my current boyfriend though, so maybe I was a little biased by now.

"Yeah, I-I remember." *Kind of.*

The thing about too many shots were that the details were fuzzy.

I'd definitely given someone a blowjob, and had got one in return, and I must've given my name in there somewhere seeing as the bloke was here. Obviously, it had to be him. I didn't have the habit of going around introducing myself to random people.

"Uh, yeah, so, the thing is…" He scratched awkwardly at the back of his neck and he kept his head bent as he shifted uncomfortably from foot to foot. "I… Oh God, I don't know how to—"

"What is it?" My forehead wrinkled in a frown. I glanced over at the register where the customer had finished paying and was putting her wallet back in her purse. My boss was still there, smiling at the woman.

The bloke in front of me seemed to go even paler, if that was even possible.

I felt sorry for him. What could possibly be so bad he seemed like he was going to faint?

"I'm HIV-positive."

The quickly-spoken words registered slowly. "What does that have to do with me?" *Oh, no, no, no.*

Dull, brown eyes glanced up before guiltily cutting away. "I'm not sure when I contracted it, but it could've been before you and I hooked up. We didn't use condoms and… well, you *swallowed*." The last word came out in such a low voice that I barely caught it.

Except I did. "Oh, my God."

"I'm so sorry!" All I could see now was a mop of

shaggy brown hair as he bowed his head as far down as possible. "I am *so* sorry."

"It's not your fault." I had to force the words out.

It was true, though.

I could've insisted on being safe; I had even put a condom packet in my pocket before going out that night. I remembered that clearly now, just in case I got lucky.

"It's okay. Can you just... go?" It wasn't okay. It wasn't okay at all.

A small, rectangular card was held out to me. "Will you let me know once you get your results? Just so I..."

I took the card from his trembling fingers. "Yeah, okay. I will."

His eyes came up to look at me one last time, then he turned and left the salon.

I stared down at the card, seeing a name, number, and e-mail that I didn't even register.

I could've contracted HIV by being careless.

And what was worse...

I could've given it to Silver.

We'd only ever used condoms when having anal sex, and Silver always swallowed when he blew me.

Oh, no!

I clapped a hand in front of my mouth, then turned tail and ran through the salon into the back.

Chloe called my name, but I had no time for her.

I slammed the door to the loo open and fell to my knees in front of the toilet. Not a moment too late, as my stomach emptied itself of the delicious breakfast Silver had made for me that very morning.

It had been too good to be true.

I was not meant to have a hot boyfriend all to myself. I'd only been with Silver for three weeks and it was already going to shit.

I might've contracted HIV.

I might've passed it on to Silver.

Silver was not going to want to stay with me once I told him.

Which led me to my current problem.

Actually *telling* him.

I had no idea how I was going to do it.

How do you tell someone you are starting to really care about that you might've given him a deadly disease?

I didn't even know how to go about this myself, let alone factor Silver into it.

"Kian? Are you all right?"

I jumped at Sun-Hi's voice and my head shot up to look at her.

She stood in the kitchen doorway, her thick, black

hair pulled back from her face and her eyes crinkled in worry.

"I'm fine." Now that was a blatant lie. If she couldn't tell the lie from my words, which she absolutely *could*, then she could tell from the way I curled in on myself on the sofa.

"Kian." Sun-Hi crossed the living room floor and sat down next to me. "I can tell something's on your mind. What's wrong?"

I looked at my hands. They rested atop my curled-up knees and they trembled.

How could I possibly tell my step-mum the truth? I hadn't known her very long, but I'd come to care for her so much. She was what a mother was supposed to be like.

Whatever I said to her, though, would get to my dad, and I'd only known him as long as I had her.

"Kian?" Sun-Hi's hand covered mine and squeezed. Her skin was darker than my pale one, thanks to her Asian genes. "Please tell me what is bothering you."

"I've done something really stupid."

Understatement of the year, much?

Safe sex campaigns were everywhere.

How could I possibly be so careless as to have unsafe sexual encounters?

I *knew* it was dangerous, that it was playing with fate.

"Did you break up with that lad you've been seeing?"

"No. He *is* probably going to break up with me though." I closed my eyes. "No, scratch that. He's *definitely* going to break up with me." Saying it hurt. So how much more would it hurt to actually hear Silver say it?

"Why?" She sounded confused. "I thought you two were doing so well."

"We were, we *are*, it's just... this bloke came to see me at work today. We hooked up once, some time ago, and now he came to tell me he's got HIV."

Sun-Hi frowned. "You used protection, didn't you?"

"Not on oral," I admitted in a low, thin voice. "I was so pissed that night. I know it's not an excuse, but it's all I've got. And if he's given it to me, then I've most likely given it to Silver." I pulled my hands out from under hers to cover my face.

"So you haven't been—" Her frown deepened.

"We haven't used protection on oral, either." It came out muffled through my hands, but fully understandable.

It was mortifying telling this to my step-mum, but

I didn't have anyone else to tell. No one who was around right now.

"If I've got it, he's got it. We've only been together three weeks, but, well…" We had an active sex life. We'd had sex before we'd even become a couple.

The odds weren't good, not good at all.

"You have to tell him, Kian." Her hands moved to squeeze my knee. "He has to know about this. He has to go get tested. *You* have to go get tested."

"I know. I just—" I did know. I knew it so well. "I just don't know how to tell him. I don't want him to break up with me."

"He might not." Her voice was so calm.

It didn't help me at all.

"Who wants to stay with the bloke who's given you HIV?" I could hear how bitter my own voice sounded.

"You might not have it, Kian. You just have to tell him so you can both get tested. The sooner you do that, the sooner you'll know. It's always better to know for sure than to put it off and keep wondering. Nothing good ever comes from that."

"Yeah. I know."

Of course Silver had to know.

I had to tell him.

It wasn't something I could put off, either.

If I'd got it from that bloke, then it'd already been

two months for me, and three weeks for Silver. Too long a time, for both of us.

"Come eat something first, Kian. It's late, so there's nothing you can do today. Get a good meal in you, then go off to tell your boyfriend. It's better to do these things on a full stomach." She smiled reassuringly and squeezed my knee one last time before getting up and heading back into the kitchen.

My hands dropped and my head tilted back to rest against the back of the sofa.

Eating wasn't a good idea. I'd probably throw it all up afterwards, but I could never say no to Sun-Hi. She'd done so much for me, welcomed me with open arms when Dad brought me home to meet her and Kasey.

I sighed deeply and unfolded myself.

Eat, and then head over to Silver's... what was I going to say?

How was I going to say it?

Silver, I'm so sorry.

CHAPTER 8

I couldn't get my hand to work.

I was supposed to knock on the door, but my hand simply wouldn't lift to do it.

I didn't know how long I stood there in frozen silence, staring at the door. I knew I should either knock or run off, but I couldn't get myself to do either.

"Kian?"

I jerked around in surprise at hearing my name, and found myself face-to-face with Damian. "Oh, Damian, hey." I shuffled uncomfortably.

He had a strap over one shoulder and I could see books peeking out of the bag resting against his upper thigh and hips. He must've been cramming until late, which wasn't that unusual, as he was enrolled in medical school. Planning to become a surgeon, even.

"Nobody home?" He looked at the door, curious.

"I don't know." I looked that way, too. My courage was still non-existent. "I haven't knocked yet."

Damian brushed past me, and he cast me an odd look on the way before trying the handle. The door opened without any resistance and it swung outwards.

He went in, but I couldn't get my feet to move.

He turned back around, eying me. "You coming in?"

I hesitated.

What would happen once I saw Silver, once I told him?

But the fact that I *had* to tell him, for his own health, made me slowly move my feet, one in front of the other, until I was inside.

I looked around, but the living room and kitchen were vacated.

Damian headed off to his own bedroom, so I toed off my shoes and walked over to Silver's door.

Once in front of that one, a sense of urgency over-came me and I knocked rapidly.

The door swung open only a moment later to

reveal Silver's broad, oh-so-very-handsome face and body.

"Hey, you." He bent down to kiss me, but pulled away quickly when I didn't reciprocate. He looked at me funnily and my chest squeezed tight in dread. "Are you all right?"

"Silver, I have to talk to you." That was a sentence shrouded with bad omens for every single person who heard it, and he clearly thought so as well, because his brows drew together in a frown.

I brushed past him into the room and sat down on his desk chair. There was no way I could sit on the bed while delivering the news—the bed I'd had such wonderful nights in the past three weeks.

Silver shut the door, then went over to sit on said bed. "What's wrong?"

He looked worried and I hated putting that expression there. It didn't belong at all. I wanted Silver to smile, to touch me and kiss me and fuck me into the mattress.

"I really don't know how to tell you this." I lowered my head to stare at my hands, which lay restlessly in my lap.

"Just spit it out," he suggested in a low voice. "It's better to rip the plaster off than to peel it off inch by inch."

Very profound and very true.

I chanced a glance up at him, meeting those grey eyes head-on for a few moments before I ducked my head again. "This bloke I pulled once some time ago came to talk to me today. He's been diagnosed with HIV. He's not sure when he contracted it, which means that I might have it, and if so—you might, too." I closed my eyes during the rant, waiting for the anger to come.

It didn't.

Instead, there was only silence.

I blinked my eyes open to look at him.

He sat calmly on the bed, gaze trained on me. The only sign that he'd actually heard what I said was the way he bit thoughtfully down on his lower lip.

"When was the last time you got tested?" He leaned back, bracing his weight on his arms.

"A while," I admitted. "Before that bloke. I didn't even remember him until he told me. I was pissed that night and feeling lonely, so I gave him a blowjob in the loo at Heaven. An unprotected blowjob."

He nodded slightly. "Okay, so—we need to get tested, then."

"We?" My eyes widened in surprise.

How could he be so calm about it?

We could've both contracted HIV.

As far as I saw it, there was major reason to panic.

"Yeah." He leaned forward again and rested his

forearms on his knees. "You and me. We'll go together."

"So, you're not—" *breaking up with me*? I couldn't get myself to finish the sentence aloud.

Silver smiled slightly. "I'm not breaking up with you. It's not *your* fault, Ki. Sometimes we do unsafe things in the heat of passion and it comes back to bite us in the arse later. We can only hope we've been lucky, in which case, we should definitely start being a lot safer."

I'd been expecting him to break it off for exposing him to the virus, and here Silver was being all zen and reasonable about it, not mentioning a break-up at all.

"I did a little research. There are several clinics we could go to tomorrow within reasonable distance that offer HIV testing." I had booted up my laptop after dinner to do said research.

I'd wanted to come prepared with an option, just in case Silver was willing to listen.

Why had I even doubted him at all?

Silver would've never broken up with me in anger. I knew that already after only three weeks together. He was always calm and collected. He usually thought things out before he acted. This wasn't any different.

Silver stood and came over to me. He crouched down and squeezed my hands in his big ones.

My restless movements instantly stopped.

"It'll be fine, Ki. No matter what, it'll be fine."

I wasn't so sure I could believe *that*, not if the tests came back positive. I didn't want to live with a life-threatening disease. I knew there were good medications and people lived a long time if they took good care of themselves nowadays, but... I didn't want to worry every single minute of every day. I didn't.

"Come on, love." Silver cupped the back of my neck, and he drew me down into a tight embrace.

I rested my face against his neck, breathing in the familiar scent of his cologne.

"I'll be fine. Don't worry until there's actually anything to worry about."

"It's hard not to." I clutched at his shoulders. "I can't believe you're so calm about this."

"Everybody takes that risk when they engage in sexual activities. It's our own fault, really, for not playing it safe. If we're lucky, this will be a lesson in being safe, if not... well, then, we have to play it safe for the rest of our lives. Something people should do anyway if they're not in a long-term monogamous relationship."

Long-term monogamous relationship... that was what I wanted with him.

I wanted it more than anything else.

It still seemed the possibility was on the table, at least for now.

I only hoped it wouldn't change if the tests turned out to be positive.

∼

THE MAIN AREAS of the flat were empty when I came home, but Chloe's shoes were carelessly deposited in the hall, so I knew she was home.

I tip-toed over to her bedroom door, knocked, then peeked in. I also knew she was alone, because there hadn't been any other shoes there besides our own.

"Hey, you." Chloe was lying on her bed reading, but now she gave me her full attention.

I went into the room and padded over to her bed, then all but fell down beside her.

She put her book down on her chest. "Where've you been all day? You got sick at work and left, so I thought I'd find you here at home. But no... you were AWOL. Are you still sick?" She brushed my fringe away from my forehead, her own creasing worriedly.

"I'm not sick. I wasn't actually *sick* at work either, not like I've got a stomach bug or something." I stared up at the ceiling. It was just as hard to tell her as it had been to tell Sun-Hi—and especially Silver.

"Then what's wrong?"

"That bloke who came to speak with me... I hooked up with him once, before Silver. And now he's HIV-positive."

She blew out a breath. "Oh, God."

"I don't think he's got anything to do with it." I took her duvet and pulled it over me. I felt cold. Cold and miserable and afraid.

"It's going to be okay." She stroked my cheek.

"What if it's not? Everyone seems to be so positive abo—oh Jesus, that's *so* the wrong word to use!" I pulled the duvet all up over my face and groaned.

"Come on. You don't have to be so *negative* just yet."

"Chloe!" I would never be able to use those two words again without being reminded of this day.

If I was positive, I would be reminded of it for the rest of my *life*.

"Sorry." I knew she was grinning, even without seeing her. "But really, there's no use whinging about it until there's something to whinge about."

I let the duvet drop to my neck so I could look up at her. She was serious again now. "I just told Silver about it."

Her eyebrows drew together. "And what'd he say?"

"He was all calm and *zen*. I'm the one who's freaking out."

"Why are you here? If he didn't take it badly, why aren't you staying the night with him, like you've done since the day I set the two of you up?" She lay down on her back beside me. Our sides touched, and her hand slid into mine.

I gripped it tightly.

"Thought it would be best to spend the night apart. I don't think I could be tempted into anything with the way I'm feeling right now, but my body's notoriously treacherous when it comes to him. I just have to be in the same room as him to be turned on."

"TMI, mate. TMI." Yet, she squeezed my hand back. "But seriously. I'm sure it'll be fine. Did you have penetrative sex with him?"

I shook my head on the pillow. "No, only oral."

"Then there's a pretty good chance that you're perfectly fine. There's less risk with oral than with anal, you know that."

I sighed, then turned over on my side and put my head on her shoulder. "Yes, but… it's still possible."

"Maybe he got it after you hooked up with him?"

"Maybe." I wasn't going to hold out hope for anything until I got my test answers back.

She put our linked hands on her stomach, while her other arm reached over to rub my upper arm.

"Are you staying with Quinn tonight?"

"No."

"Is she coming over here?"

"No. Why?"

Her denial to both made me feel extremely relieved right then. "Can I sleep here with you tonight? I don't want to be alone."

She stopped rubbing my arm and instead slid it over my back to hug me tightly. "Of course you can."

"You're my best friend. You know that, right?" I'd never told her in words before, but I was in a mellow enough mood to do it now. I'd never felt like this before, not even when my own mother had dusted her hands of me. Not this worried, this afraid, this anxious.

"Yeah, du-uh." She chuckled and hugged me even tighter. "And just for your information, you're mine, too."

I knew that already, but it still lifted my mood just a tiniest bit.

"Try to sleep some. At this time tomorrow, you won't have to worry anymore. Then you can cuddle up in bed with your bloke, instead of with me."

I didn't answer, only settled down.

My mind was on overdrive, but I was tired. It had

been an eventful day, to say the least, and I had to get up early for us to go take our tests.

Safe to say, it didn't take me long to fall asleep.

"I'm sorry, Silver." I looked over at him with a solemn expression.

His hand stopped whatever it was he drew in his sketchbook as he looked at me. "For what?"

"For being able to get my results today, while you have to wait for yours." I'd been able to take a rapid HIV test, as it had been about two months since my exposure.

It had only been three weeks for Silver, so his blood sample had to be sent in to a laboratory for testing.

"Waiting is the worst."

"Stop fretting." He ran the back of his hand down my cheek. "If your test is good, then most likely, mine will be as well."

I liked the sound of that.

Not because Silver was simply assuming his test would be fine, but because that actually meant that Silver had only been with me since the last time he got tested.

I leaned over to rest my head on his shoulder.

"You are so wonderful." I looped my arm around his loosely, careful not to cut off his movement as he went back to sketching.

I looked at it and saw the very room we were sitting in reflected on paper. "That's brilliant."

Silver chuckled, but he didn't say anything. His hand kept moving over the paper, adding the smallest detail to the drawing. It never ceased to amaze me just how attentive he was to detail when he drew—or especially when he tattooed.

A door *swooshed* open, bringing my head up in curiosity.

The doctor who'd seen to my test appeared and my stomach dropped in nervousness.

"Well, I'm up." I squeezed Silver's arm tightly for a moment, gathering my courage, before I got up to follow the doctor.

I glanced back at Silver.

Steel-grey eyes met my own calmly.

I took a deep breath, calming myself down, and then stepped into the office, ready to hear my answer.

CHAPTER 9

"*Y*ou know what?"

I stretched out sideways on the sofa and rested my feet across Silver's lap. His hands instantly started massaging my feet as his head turned to face me.

"What?"

"When that bloke told me he was HIV-positive, I was sure that this was it. That this thing between us, new as it is, was over already. I felt like it was too good to be true, that it certainly had to have an expiration date, you know, but I wasn't prepared for it to happen so soon."

He frowned. "Have I ever given you a reason to believe that there *was* an expiration date? That this was only temporary?"

"No." I met his gaze head-on. "You haven't. You've been nothing but wonderful. Which is why I've kind of been waiting for the other shoe to drop, you know? I've never been in a relationship before. Never had anyone interested in a relationship with *me*. Not even my mum wants to have a relationship with me."

"You can't judge anyone from your mum, Kian. If anyone should be in the loony bin, it's her. Your dad came back once you were of age, once she couldn't keep him away any longer. Now *that's* what counts."

I sat up and bent forward, into his personal space. I brushed my lips softly over his before smiling at him. "Of course that counts. It counts a lot. I just... I can't believe I've been so lucky, to get *you*."

"I'm hardly a catch," he snorted.

I swatted playfully at his arm. "You sort of are."

"I think *you* are." It was his turn to kiss me. His kiss was harder, deeper, with a touch of tongue. It made my whole body tingle. "I think you're a great catch."

I wiggled around until I could properly straddle his thighs.

Silver's arm instantly slid down my sides to settle on my arse.

"Careful," I murmured, leaning forward until our

lips hovered only inches apart. "They advise against shagging until your test results come back."

"We already know my test will be negative." His voice was soft. "You're the only one I've been with since the last time I got tested."

"When was that?" I slid my arms over his shoulders and let one hand tangle in his black hair.

"A long time." His eyes were sincere when he looked into mine. "At least half a year. Probably longer. I can't remember exactly."

I liked hearing that; there was no other way about it. I liked hearing how whoever he'd been with last hadn't been important enough for him to remember. Liked hearing he hadn't been with anyone for such a long time and when he chose to finally be with someone again, he'd chosen me.

That was an ego boost, for sure.

"Still, we should do as they advised and wait until your results get back."

He groaned low in his throat, then flipped us over so that I was on my back and he pressed me down into the soft fabric of the sofa. "I don't want to wait."

I laughed breathlessly as he sucked on the thin skin right underneath my jaw. It turned into a moan when he started sucking, licking, kissing, and biting his way down my neck.

Thinking was impossible when he did that.

All I could do was feel it, and enjoy what his attention always did to my body. It started a slow burn that seemed to spread out to my limbs so that all I could do was hold on to him as he did his magic.

No one got me as hot and wired as Silver.

Nothing else seemed to exist besides him: his body and his mouth and his hands. They did such wonderful things to me, they fired my body up like no one else had ever done before, and the whole world disappeared around me—

Until I snapped back to attention by the opening of the front door.

Silver lifted his head away from my skin and I couldn't stop the slight sound of disappointment that left me. I arched my neck back and saw Damian and Josh looking back at me.

"Sorry." Josh avoided my gaze. "We didn't mean to interrupt."

While Josh sounded surprised, but pleasant, Damian frowned. "You have a room," he shot at Silver.

"We were getting to it in a minute." Silver flashed a grin at him, causing Damian to roll his eyes as he turned away.

Josh smiled sheepishly before following towards Damian's bedroom.

"Hey—whoa!" I wrapped my arms around Silver's neck as he easily scooped me up into his arms. "What're you doing?"

Silver headed towards his own bedroom. "What do you think?" He carried me easily, like I weighed nothing, before depositing me on his bed. "Lay down comfortably and don't move."

I did as told and stretched out. I watched as Silver sat down on his desk chair and flipped open an A3 sketchbook. "Are you going to draw me?"

He nodded. "You mind?" His gaze was intense as he focused on me.

"No. Not at all." Silver could definitely do all he wanted. I would model for him naked, if that was what he wanted of me.

That was actually quite a good idea. But it would have to wait for another day, when we weren't under advice to cease sexual activities until the HIV test came back.

Mine might've been negative, and his most likely would be, but we could never be too sure. We'd agreed to play it safe from now on, although if we were going to be exclusive... well, if we were, then the condoms would eventually come off altogether.

It was a while off still, but I couldn't help the thought.

One thing at a time, though.

First, we had to assure ourselves that we'd skipped this crisis. When that was done, then we could move ahead again.

I didn't mind taking it slow.

We *had* only been together for three weeks, after all.

～

"MY BALLS ARE TURNING BLUE."

I looked down at my crotch just for emphasis.

"Oh, please. As if that's even possible." Chloe bumped me with her shoulder.

"No, *you* come on. You're not a complete lesbian. *You* know how blokes get when they can't get off. I'm walking around with a constant stiffy here."

She laughed. Out loud. The bitch. "Tough to be you, Kian."

"It is. I haven't had sex in a *week*."

She snorted. "Come on. You've gone without a heck of a lot longer before."

I leaned over the table to flick her hand.

She pulled it back with a grimace and glared at me.

"Not when I've been in a relationship with possibly the hottest lad *ever*. Do you have any idea how tough it is to be around him and not jump him?"

Her grimace turned into a completely unimpressed expression. "As you so clearly put it, I'm not a complete lesbian, so yes, I know just how good-looking Silver is. If I hadn't had a girlfriend, I would've tried to rip his clothes off myself. I certainly wouldn't have put the two of you together. But I *do* have a girlfriend, so you were in luck."

"Ha. Ha." I sat back in my seat and stabbed my fork into my salad.

She laughed harder. "If you're so desperate for it, why can't you just have sex? Use condoms and you'll be fine."

"I told you already, they say to abstain from it until the test results are back."

"Shouldn't they be back by now though?"

I stabbed some more at my salad. "You would think. They like to take their time."

"Well, at least you know you'll get to have lots of sex once the results do come back."

"That doesn't make me feel any better. I swear, my dick's going to be permanently hard and my balls are going to fall off if this continues."

"Stop being so dramatic." She waved her fork at me before taking a bite of her own salad. "It won't be long now. Why don't you just wank off?"

"I *do*. But it's not enough." How could I not need

more when close to Silver? It was impossible not to get horny when he touched or kissed me.

She snorted into her drink. "We should go out tonight. Get your mind off of your dick."

"It's impossible to get my mind off my dick. It's *always* hard."

"Yeah, yeah. I don't need to hear about your prowess. Leave that for your boyfriend; I'm sure he'll appreciate it a lot more than I will."

"Oh, he does," I promised her with a wink. "He sure does."

She only rolled her eyes.

SILVER and I met outside his building, totally by accident, but a welcome one as such.

I didn't get a chance to say anything though, before he dragged me into a hot and heavy kiss.

I wrapped my arms around his neck and let him steer me so my back was up against the wall beside the front door.

His whole body moulded against mine and covered me completely, since he was so much bigger than me. I loved it. There was no other way about it.

"What was that for?" I asked breathlessly, when he pulled back from the kiss.

"Got my results back." A grin spread slowly on his lips and his eyes twinkled. "Negative. Which means…" His hand travelled down my front suggestively.

My cock instantly went from half-hard to rock-hard. "That is the best thing I've heard this past *week*." Abstaining from sex wasn't hard when I'd been single with no prospects, but when I had a hot boyfriend, it'd been hell. All I'd wanted was to get naked with him and the fact that I couldn't… well, we better be safe from now on, because I wasn't about to go through that again.

Both his hands came up to cup my cheeks. His grin had turned into a soft smile. It made my knees weak, and if he hadn't kept me pressed up against the wall, I was pretty sure I would melt into a puddle of goo at his feet.

He bent his head down to nuzzle his slightly-stubbled cheek against my smooth one. "I like you so much, Kian."

"I like you a lot, too." Might even be in love with him, after only a month together. But maybe it was too early to voice those feelings just yet?

"I'm meeting my brother for dinner tomorrow." He pulled back again so he could look at my face.

I had a thought as to where he was going with that statement.

"I want you to come with me."

I swallowed. "You want me to meet your brother?" That made me equally happy and terrified. His brother was his family, the one he was closest to, and meeting him would be a big deal, a big turning point in our relationship.

Was this the point where it went from being just-getting-to-know-each-other to really-serious?

"He wants to meet you, too." He still smiled softly.

"I-I'd love to meet him." I tried to return it, but it came out strained because of the bout of nerves that bloomed.

His thumbs stroked over my cheekbones. "Don't be nervous, babe. He'll love you."

The pet name washed over me, soothing some of the nervousness. "I hope so."

"I know so." He kissed me again, not as hard and heavy as the first kiss, but softer, sweeter. It didn't dull my desire any. In fact, it only made it worse. I ached to feel him closer, to feel his skin, to feel him fuck me into the mattress.

"Inside?" I got out between kisses. "Bed? Now? Please?" I wasn't beyond begging. If it got me what I wanted, what I needed, I was all okay with doing it.

"Yes." He nipped at my lower lip before drawing

back. He reached into his pocket, and for a moment, I thought he was adjusting himself, but then he drew a box up to show me. "I got us these."

A packet of condoms.

Oh, yeah.

CHAPTER 10

"**S**o what do you do, Kian?"

I fumbled nervously with my menu. "I'm a hairdresser."

We'd just sat down at our reserved—Vincent's doing, not ours—table at a fancy restaurant, and I hadn't even had a chance to peruse the menu itself. The fact that I was a nervous wreck likely had a lot to do with that.

Vincent nodded.

He looked kind of like Silver: same facial build and same dark hair, but otherwise, they weren't alike at all. Vincent was tall and toned, though Silver was wider, and Vincent was preppy and clear-cut, whereas his brother was covered in tattoos and wore simple tees and ripped jeans. His hair was combed just so, while Silver's faux-hawk was styled messy. And instead of grey eyes, his were dark.

And he was older, obviously. What had Silver said? There were eleven years or so between them? Which meant this man was thirty. He looked good, but way too preppy and clear-cut for my tastes. I longed to muss up that finely-combed hair and add highlights to it, but something told me that wasn't his style.

"What do you do?" I asked it just to keep the conversation going—but I was also curious, because Silver hadn't actually told me much about his brother.

"I'm a psychiatrist."

"Oh." My turn to nod.

What more did I say?

I didn't know if I could ask any more, not concerning his career, with confidentiality and all of that stuff in the way. I didn't have any personal experience with psychiatrists or psychiatry in general.

I turned my head to look at Silver, who smiled slightly. It didn't seem like he knew what to say, either.

It was awkward, to say the least.

The waiter appeared to take our drink orders, and I finally got to look at my menu properly once he promised to be back in a little while.

Once he'd been back to take the food orders, I excused myself to go to the toilets.

I stared at myself in the mirror.

Get it together.

This is Silver's brother.

You can be a lot *more sociable than you've been till now.*

Maybe I was this awkward *because* it was Silver's brother? I wanted him to like me. He was Silver's family, after all.

I splashed some water in my face, making sure not to ruin the make-up around my eyes. I hadn't toned it down—I'd done my make-up exactly like I used to. I hadn't wanted to appear like anyone I wasn't the first time I met Vincent.

Patting my face dry with some paper, I took a deep breath, then made my way back out into the restaurant.

I could see Vincent and Silver bent in close together, and the closer I got, the more I could hear of their conversation.

"He's different," Vincent said, but he didn't sound judgmental. I guess that was a plus.

"He is. I like him a lot."

My heart squeezed at Silver's admission.

"He's not at all like—"

"No he's not." Silver interrupted Vincent there, and his words were final.

Curiosity flamed up in me. I wondered who Vincent had been talking about. Who wasn't I at all alike?

"Have you told him about—?"

"No." Another curt interruption. "Not yet. I can't. How can I possibly tell him something like that?"

"The same way you told me, and Damian."

Silver started shaking his head and he sat back properly on his chair. His eyes fell on me, and I smiled widely as I took the last few steps over to my chair.

I tried not to worry about him keeping secrets from me—it'd only been a month, after all—and so I gave him another smile.

"You all right?"

I nodded. "Yeah. Are you?" He seemed a bit out of it. It must've been because of whatever Vincent had been hinting about. Or not so much hinting as directly saying it and being interrupted before he actually managed to finish off his sentence.

"Yeah, yeah."

Vincent glanced between us, but his focus eventually settled on me.

I swallowed, my nervousness ratting up again.

He has to like me; he just has to.

"Do you have any family, Kian?"

"Yes, I do." That was a non-answer if I'd ever heard any, so I hurried to tell him about my dad, step-mother, and my little brother. I left my mother out of it; she wasn't important. Never had been, never would be again.

I was lucky to have found a proper family with my dad. And I could make my own, too... If things did work out with Silver, he'd be my family as well.

I hoped it did.

Work out, that was.

Dinner was delivered and my nervousness disappeared little by little.

Vincent was soft-spoken, kind, and friendly. He made a point of asking me questions, and neither he nor Silver left me out of their conversations.

"That went well, I think?" I stepped in close to Silver as we parted from his brother.

He bobbed his head. "He likes you."

"I like him, too. He's very nice."

Silver smiled. "Yeah, he is. Though he doesn't take any crap, either. At least not mine, when I lived with him."

I cocked my head to the side. "I can't imagine you giving him much crap."

"I did. I was a right little shit." He grinned, which told me he was joking.

I laughed and slid my arm around his elbow. "Next time, you're meeting my family."

"Now, that's something to be nervous about." He pretended to shudder. "There's three of them."

"Yeah, and one's a ten-year-old little boy. I don't think he poses much of a threat."

"Oh, I don't know. Ten-year-olds can be quite perceptive."

I laughed as I patted his arm. "Don't worry, babe, I'll be there to protect you."

He extricated his arm from mine and instead wrapped it around my shoulders, drawing me in close to his side.

I wasn't complaining *at all* about this new position.

"Come home with me?" He kissed the top of my head.

"I was kind of counting on that." I wrapped my own arm around his waist, squeezing him tight.

"MY BROTHER *FANCIES* YOU!"

I bent over laughing the moment we were inside the door. My sides hurt: that was how hard I was laughing.

Silver wasn't as amused. He pushed me over onto

the sofa, then dropped down beside me and proceeded to tickle me, which caused laughter of another kind.

"I yield, I yield!"

I was on my back, he was braced above me, and we stared at each other for a long moment.

A teasing grin slowly spread on his lips. "Your brother *is* quite cute."

I stabbed a finger against his chest. "He's ten. And my brother."

"And he, apparently, *fancies* me."

"That boost your confidence?" I chuckled. "A ten-year old with a crush on you?"

"Maybe it does." He winked at me, then promptly sat back and pulled me up with him. "They start early nowadays. I did *not* fancy people when I was ten. I was probably pulling pigtails back then."

"So when were you aware of your sexuality?"

He stared down at me. "You knew you were gay when you were ten?"

"Well…" I couldn't actually remember what I did when I was ten. Probably just trying to stay out of my mother's way. "Okay, I guess they start early. I had no idea I was gay when I was ten. I had no idea Kasey was gay until his face turned bright red when you spoke to him."

Silver chuckled at the memory. "He's sweet."

"How can you know? We didn't get a word out of him after that." I leaned in to kiss his neck. "I hardly even saw his face, except when he snuck glances at you."

"Aren't you happy to have such a hot boyfriend? Even your own brother can't keep his eyes off me."

"Conceited, much?" I stabbed a finger against his chest again.

He grabbed my hand and fanned my fingers out, so my palm rested against his chest instead of my index finger.

All joking was put aside when he leaned down to kiss me.

"You realise we've been together for over two months by now?" It was an incredible thing—butter-flies fluttered around my gut just at the simple thought.

He smiled. "I do. It's like time's just flown by."

"I know, right. These two months with you have been pretty amazing."

He kissed me again and I moved to straddle his lap. He thrust his hand down my jeans, but they were as tight as ever, so he had to unzip them with his free one. Which he did expertly. And then my jeans and boxers were pulled down the tiniest bit, just so my cock came free from the confinements.

"What about your flatmates?" I murmured against his lips.

"They're not here, are they?" His big hand squeezed me wonderfully. All my nerve endings felt like they were on fire.

I ran my hands over his neck, around, and up into his hair. I grabbed onto the longest strands, needing something to keep me grounded and from coming the moment he stroked me.

"I liked your family," he murmured then. "They seemed kind. They were welcoming."

I peered at him through narrowed eyes. "Why are you talking about my family *now*?" There was something majorly wrong about that subject when he was wanking me off.

"Just wanted you to know, babe." His free hand settled on the small of my back, thumb caressing me softly.

His other hand sped up on my cock and I could only moan in answer.

I dropped my head forward, down on his shoulder. My hips bucked with his movements, begging for him to just get me off right *now*.

And he delivered.

He stroked me, changing between slow and quick, and just squeezing me.

It didn't take me long.

He knew exactly what I liked—and how to bring me over the edge.

I came with a long, drawn-out groan. Upon opening my eyes, which had closed somewhere in there, I saw my semen trickle from the head of my softening cock and down over his fingers.

"Want me to do you?" I could feel he was hard against my bum.

"Nah. You can reciprocate later." He gently pushed me off of him and stood. "I'll go wash up."

I tucked myself back into my underwear and jeans and zipped them up properly.

I'd just put my head back on the sofa when Damian's bedroom door opened and he himself stepped out. I sent a quick thanks to the heavens that he hadn't emerged a couple minutes earlier.

Silver came back out of the bathroom, but his smile faded once he got a good look at Damian's face. I understood—he didn't look so good.

"Hey, mate. All right?"

Damian glanced towards the kitchen. "Where's Josh?"

"Not here. I thought he was in there with you." Silver pointed at Damian's door.

Damian shook his head slowly, looking lost for a second before he pressed his hands to his face.

"Mate, what's wrong?" I could tell Silver was worried.

I was, too, and I didn't know Damian *that* well. But I had never seen him like this before. He was usually so cool and aloof.

"I pushed him away." The words were low: so low that they almost didn't reach me where I sat in the sofa.

Silver's brows drew together in a frown. "What'd you mean?"

"I physically pushed him." Damian let his hands drop and there was an emotion in his eyes there, but one I didn't know him well enough to decipher. "It's in four days, and I just realised it. He came upon me and I *pushed* him."

Silver's face right then reminded me of how cartoon characters got a light-bulb over their head once something dawned on them. "You forgot the date?"

"Yeah. I was freaking out." Damian wrapped his arms around himself, as if he was cold—or extremely uncomfortable. "I still am, a little bit. And he had to come in at that exact moment, and he was just being worried, like, and I pushed him away."

I didn't see the big problem. What was a little push? Sure, it might've angered me if Silver had pushed me, but I would've got over it once I calmed down. "Just ring him, mate. Explain that it was a shitty time, and apologise. I'm sure it'll be fine."

He'd started shaking his head before I'd even finished. "You don't understand." He was back to pressing his hands to his face. More specifically, his eyes. Maybe he was fighting tears. "What I just did… it's bad. So bad."

"Josh's a sweet bloke. Surely, he'll understand you didn't mean anything by it." I was sure my frown matched Silver's by now.

Damian cast a look at Silver, who gazed back at him. "You should go speak to him in person. He probably went home to his mum's. He hasn't got anywhere else to go, has he?"

"No."

"The quicker you go talk to him, the quicker this'll be solved. Nothing like this has happened before, so if you apologise—and explain—I'm sure Josh will understand. If anyone should understand your feelings about your past, it's him. You need to *tell* him. You should've told him long before October came around." Silver was almost lecturing him. No, scratch that, he *was* lecturing him.

"I've been so busy, I wasn't aware of the dates. That they were getting so close to-to—"

I had to admit it; I was completely lost.

What the hell were they on about?

I got the whole part about pushing Josh away, but close to what? What was so special around this time?

"I remember around this time last year," Silver said. "We'd met only a month and a half before. I knew something was up with you, but I had no idea what. And I didn't feel like I knew you enough to ask. But when you finally told me, I understood what it was all about. So will Josh."

"No, Silver." He was frustrated: that much I could tell from his voice and his fidgeting body language. "You don't get it. I did something bad, and that will affect him. You know that borderliners have a black-and-white thinking pattern. I might've been white— but now I'm going to be all black."

Huh?

I was very officially lost—to the point I couldn't find my way back into the conversation *at all*.

"You've been together for two and a half months. Surely that can't apply to you anymore?" Silver frowned again now.

I knew I did, too, but that was because I was completely lost as to the subtext of the conversation.

Silver was just plain confused.

"It applies to everyone. A single little word can do it. And I physically *pushed* him away from me. He fell because of me. And I told him I needed to be alone.

That's more than enough reason for his thoughts to switch around to the other opposite."

"Go talk to him *now*." Silver clapped him on the shoulder. "If it is that bad, you can't waste a bloody second, D. Go to him, tell him everything, no matter how fucking hard it is. You managed to tell me. Surely you can tell him."

Damian didn't seem so sure of that.

CHAPTER 11

"*W*hat was that all about?" I asked once Damian had left the flat.

Silver dragged his hands across his face without answering.

"That whole conversation went way over my head."

"Everything?"

"Well, I got the fact that he pushed Josh. But I don't understand why it's such a big deal. It wasn't like he *hurt* him. And what kind of important date is it he forgot about? What's so important about this month?"

Silver rolled his head to the side, where it rested against the back of the sofa. "Damian's got a traumatic past. I'm talking *very* traumatic here, like Josh's past, but they haven't had the same experiences. Something you never recover from. Something we all have in common, I guess." The last part came as a muttered add-on.

I stared at him. What had happened in his past to make him say something like that? What did he have in common with Damian and Josh?

"Is it something you can tell me about? Or have you been sworn to secrecy?"

He focused back on me. "Not really. It's just never been a topic that's ever come up before. You know Damian used to live with his uncle and aunt, right?"

Well, I hadn't known that, but I had heard mention of them, so I nodded.

"That's because his whole family's dead."

"What happened to them?" I curled my legs under me and folded my hands in my lap, giving him my full attention.

"It was a, uh, murder-suicide. His mum did it."

My eyes widened in shock. I didn't even have words. How could I possibly have anything to say after such a horrifying story? I didn't even have details and I found it traumatic just to hear about it. What must he feel like, having experienced it... or had he?

"Where was Damian?"

"He was there. She thought he was dead, and so she killed herself last."

"Oh my god." That was all I could articulate. My own mother seemed rather sane and nice at the moment. She'd never once hurt me, though I reckoned neglect was hurtful in itself?

At least I'd never been physically hurt.

"Yeah. It's tragic. And the anniversary's in a few days. He's always a mess this time of year." Silver sighed, then put one hand on my folded knee and squeezed.

I wanted to ask what'd happened to him, but he'd never mentioned it to me before, and it hadn't been a part of the conversation he was explaining to me. So I didn't dare ask. I didn't want to be shut out.

If he wanted to share, he would, eventually, without me prying into it.

"And what about Josh? Why was pushing him away so bad?"

"I told you Josh is borderline. How he's got difficulties controlling his emotions. Well, it's a lot more than that, but that's the most obvious trait of it." Silver turned his head to stare up at the ceiling.

His hand didn't leave my knee, though, which was nice.

"Another part is this black-and-white thinking. Things are either all good or all bad, and just the tiniest little thing can switch that perceptive. To Josh, Damian's been something good, but if Damian pushed him and told him he needed to be alone…"

He sighed again, even more heavily this time. "If it'd happened to you or me, we would've been hurt, maybe a little angry, but it would've passed quickly. But for Josh… it's all blown out of proportion with him. Something like that sends people with border-line into a tailspin. For Josh, likely right into self-harm and depression and thinking that Damian doesn't want him anymore."

I digested what he'd just told me. It was a lot of information, but it *did* give me a bit of a clearer picture of the situation.

A more *dire* picture.

"How do you know so much about it? Is it from knowing Josh?"

"The fact that I know it at all is because of him, yeah, but back when Damian first met him and Josh revealed he was borderline, I asked Vincent about it. He's actually Josh's psychiatrist, which is quite a coincidence. Anyway, I asked him generally about borderline personality disorder, since that was before I even knew they were connected. He told me a lot of the general things about borderlines—and it applies to Josh, it really does."

I chewed lightly on the inside of my cheek. "It

sounds horrible. To live like that. With emotions so out of control."

Silver smiled sadly. "It's who he is. He doesn't know any different, I reckon."

He might be right about that.

I didn't have personal experience with mental illness. I wasn't so close to Josh that I'd experienced anything odd about him, either. Maybe odd wasn't the right word to use, considering, but I didn't know what else to call it either.

I leaned into Silver, resting my cheek against his chest.

His arms wrapped around me tightly.

Again, I was flushed with curiosity over what he'd hinted at in his own life, but he wasn't speaking, so I didn't either.

Instead, we just sat there.

I didn't know for how long.

All I knew was that I'd fallen into a doze when the front door slammed open.

I sat up with a start, and Silver jerked awake, too.

Damian strode into the flat, and it was obvious that nothing had been resolved with Josh.

"Did you get to talk to him?" Silver turned onto his side on the sofa so he could look at Damian properly.

He shook his head. "He wasn't there. His mum

wasn't, either. I tried ringing him, too, but he doesn't answer." His breathing was heavy and now I knew he was fighting tears. I'd never seen him so upset before and it was a little unsettling. I'd always seen Damian as calm and stoic, ever since I'd met him.

"Maybe he'll have calmed down by tomorrow?" Silver suggested hesitantly.

Damian shook his head again. "I'm going to bed."

I watched his back disappear into his dark bedroom.

When he softly closed the door, I turned to exchange a look with Silver.

He was troubled, worried about his best friend.

I leaned into him again, and his arms once again wrapped around me. I didn't know what to say, and he didn't either, so we didn't say anything at all.

THREE DAYS LATER, I jerked awake by someone screaming.

I noticed blurredly that Silver was also sitting up next to me, but in the next moment, he was out of the bed and out of the room.

I hurried after him, still half-asleep, but also a lot worried.

The door to Damian's bedroom was wide open, and someone still screamed in there.

Silver switched on the lights and I saw Damian leaning over Josh's thrashing form on the bed, yelling his name.

"Get it off me, get it off me, get it off me!" Josh clawed at the shirt he was wearing. There were dark patches of sweat all over it.

I was surprised to even see Josh around, least of all in Damian's bed. I knew Damian had gone to Bristol to talk to him yesterday morning, but I hadn't known they were back—and apparently together again.

Damian helped Josh out of his shirt, and now my eyes nearly bugged out of my head for another reason.

Josh's arms—and I meant *all* of his arms—were covered in scars.

When the shirt was off, Josh drew his knees up under him, bent over to rest his head against the sheets, then he wrapped his arms over his head as he rocked back and forth. He was trembling, still crying, though at least the screaming had stopped.

"Do you want us to do anything, D?" Silver asked. His hands clenched and unclenched. He obviously wanted to do something, but he wasn't sure what.

I was still horrified by the sight of Josh's arms and I couldn't quite stop my gaze from returning to them.

"I don't know." Damian's whole demeanour shook, not just his voice.

"You want me to call Vincent?" Silver took a step closer, head cocked slightly, curiously.

"No, no." Damian shook his head quickly. "I've got it. Thanks though."

"Don't hesitate to tell me if you change your mind. If he doesn't calm down." Silver reached out to squeeze Damian's shoulder, then he turned to put a hand on the small of my back as he led me out of the room.

I glanced back at Josh.

He was still curled in on himself, rocking back and forth.

"Will he be okay?"

Silver only shook his head.

"Hey, Josh. It was just a dream," I heard Damian say before Silver closed the door after us.

I didn't say anything else until we were back in Silver's bed. Silver lay down on his back, but I couldn't. So I sat cross-legged, reached over to turn on the lamp and looked down at him.

"That was—I don't have words for what that was." I could still see Josh's arms in my mind, and the way he'd curled in on himself and rocked back and forth. He hadn't even reacted to Silver and I being in the room.

"His arms…" I'd never seen so many scars in my life. There hadn't been a single piece of unscarred skin.

"Babe, come here." Silver held his arms out wide.

I shook my head. "I don't think I can sleep yet. My heart's still racing after that wake-up." The way he'd screamed… "What kind of dreams causes those kinds of reactions?"

"Not dreams. Memories posing as dreams."

I gazed down at him.

He looked right back at me.

"I have to go to the loo." I left the room quickly.

Once in the bathroom, I turned the tap on and splashed cold water in my face. I didn't know what exactly had happened to Josh, but after tonight… I knew it was bad—really bad. For him to wake up screaming like that, and to cut his arms up so badly, it couldn't be anything but horrifying.

I went back to the bedroom.

Silver was on his side now, turned away from my side.

I shimmied into bed and then turned my head to look at his back. There wasn't a single piece of uninked skin on his back. I had seen the back tattoo plenty of times, but I'd never given it much thought.

"I didn't have a pleasant childhood," I said in a low voice. I wasn't sure if he'd already fallen asleep or not, but I had things to say and I needed to get them out. "I wasn't abused, not in the sense of the word, not like how you think when you hear it. I was neglected. My mum didn't give a shit about me. It was all about her and her drinking and her drug use and her boyfriends."

My eyes roamed Silver's back. It was mostly black and shaded, but the roses tattooed on his skin were a dark red. I cocked my head more to the side and saw to my wonder that there was writing there, across his back, right under his shoulder blades. The letters went so well with the rest of the tattoo that I hadn't seen them before.

But the letters were there.

R.I.P.

"I had to take care of myself. Sometimes, she couldn't even take care of *her*self, you know. Sometimes, I got more attention from her boyfriends than I liked, but they never touched me. I don't know if that was because of her, because she'd told them to stay away, or because they weren't really that into boys after all, but I got some creepy looks."

Who did he know that had died?

Surely when he had his entire backside covered in

ink, those words weren't just there for effect. Surely it had to mean something?

"I guess I was lucky, after all. I didn't feel lucky, growing up, having to deal with her passed out or ignoring me if she was alert. But hearing what happened to Damian, and knowing something real bad has happened to Josh... I guess I have been lucky."

Silver flopped over on his back, grey eyes gazing at me. He extended one arm and I quickly scooted over to rest my head on his shoulder.

"Something's happened to me, too. Something bad, something that could've, perhaps, been avoided. I know I was on Damian to tell Josh about *his* past, but I can't tell you about mine, Ki. Not now, not yet." His hand carded through my hair, his fingertips massaging my scalp gently.

"It's okay. I wasn't telling you about my past to make you open up about yours."

"Mine's a bit more *recent* than for the rest of you." I reckoned he was referring to me, Josh, and Damian.

"It's *okay*," I stressed. "I just needed to get that out. I wasn't trying to make you feel guilty or anything. I know my experiences aren't anything to Damian's or Josh's, or likely yours, but I just needed to tell you about them."

"Your experiences matter just as much as anyone

else's. Even if they're not as bad, they're still bad for you, who experienced it."

A chuckle escaped me at that. "How profound."

"I am that sometimes."

I lifted my head off his shoulder so I could kiss him. It was just a chaste kiss, no tongue, but it was nice nonetheless.

"Can we please sleep now?" He seemed tired— and not like it was because it was late, but more in general.

Maybe he had something in common with Josh's past?

Maybe tonight's events had reminded him of something? He'd been perfectly happy when we'd gone to bed.

"Yeah." Another chaste kiss, then I put my head back down on his shoulder. My heart was still raced faster than normal, but it was slowly calming down. Much thanks to him.

I eventually fell asleep, but awoke groggily for a minute when he rolled me away from him. I felt the bed shift as he got up, heard him leave the room.

It'd been a while since I'd caught him having bad dreams now. I hadn't actually caught him now, either, but he only ever left me alone in bed when he had nightmares and couldn't sleep.

What happened to you, Silver?

The sight of his tattoo flashed before my mind.

Someone was dead.

And their death had left its scar on Silver.

I just didn't know when or how or what it all meant to Silver.

Two months we've been together.

It wasn't overly long, even though I was entirely used to having him in my life and couldn't imagine said life without him anymore.

I hoped that he'd trust me one day. That one day he'd be comfortable enough to tell me what plagued him at night.

CHAPTER 12

"Silver, what are you doing for Christmas?"

When only silence met my question, I looked over at Silver and bumped his shoulder with my own. "Hey?"

He glanced at me. "Nothing special." He then looked back down at his own hands.

I frowned. "Are you celebrating with Vincent?"

"He's going back home to celebrate with our parents this year."

Something bothered him; I could tell from both the subdued tone of his voice and the way he wouldn't meet my gaze. Why didn't he go back to his hometown with Vincent, to celebrate Christmas with his parents?

"Didn't you get time off from work?" It was the only explanation I could think of. If I couldn't have celebrated Christmas with my family because of obligations at work, I would've been in a right state, too.

"I would've, I guess." He shrugged. "I just didn't want to."

I blinked. "So you're going to spend Christmas alone?" That was *not* acceptable. "Why don't you celebrate with me?"

He raised his head again and arched his eyebrows. "Aren't you celebrating at your dad's place?"

"Yeah, but you can come too. They won't mind. Kasey *loves* you, and I mean that literally." I flashed him a grin.

It was cute the way Kasey lost the ability to speak or make eye contact whenever I brought Silver around with me. It wasn't like a ten-year old could steal my boyfriend from me, so it was all innocent fun.

"It's your first year celebrating with your dad." He frowned. "I don't want to impose on that."

"It's the first year we're together, too," I pointed out. "I want to celebrate with you, too, if I can." I'd simply expected him to go home to his parents for

Christmas. "I know they won't mind. They really do like you."

"You sure about that, Ki?" He didn't seem sure at all.

"Come on, love. They like you. I sure as hell like you."

Sun-Hi was just as warm and kind towards Silver as she was to me.

My dad was harder to read, but he always tried to include Silver in every conversation, so I took that as a sign that he liked him, too.

And not to mention Kasey, who was all but drooling over Silver every chance he got.

"Please, babe. Come celebrate Christmas with me. With us."

This Christmas was turning out to be the best one ever. My first Christmas with my dad and my step-mum and little brother. And if Silver said yes, then it would also be my first Christmas with my first boyfriend. I had a real family for the first time in my life—and an amazing boyfriend.

"Fine." Silver pretended to roll his eyes in exasperation, but the smile directed at me gave him away. "I'll celebrate Christmas with you."

I let out a delighted laugh and moved over to straddle his lap. "I know it's still almost a month away, but we're going to have the best Christmas."

His smile faded a bit. "Yeah." It wasn't convincing in the least.

Was it the thought of not celebrating with his family that made him sad?

"You can go celebrate with your family next year. If we're still together, maybe we can do so together?" I cupped the side of his face in one palm, letting my thumb stroke over his cheekbone.

It didn't seem to lift his sad mood any.

"Yeah, maybe we will."

His hands travelled up my thighs, then slipped under my shirt.

I drew in a breath at his cool hands against my skin, but knowing what they could do to me kept me from moving away from him.

I grinned and let my own arms drop to his lap. I undid his jeans and thrust one inside, feeling his flaccid cock against my fingers. It would harden up in no time, that was for sure.

Only the front door opened and Damian trudged in, looking just as sad as Silver had minutes earlier, and dejected.

"You're home early, mate."

Damian's attention was drawn to us, and he normally would've turned away instantly at seeing the state we were in, but this time, he didn't.

That was the most telling sign that something was *wrong*.

"Hey." Silver removed his hands from me and my shirt fell back down to cover me properly.

I took my own hands out from his jeans, making sure to make him decent as well before I looked back at Damian.

"Josh's in the hospital." It came out in a low voice.

"Hospital? He left a few hours ago to go to the cinema." I'd personally told him goodbye. He'd seemed excited about going out with his mate.

"And now he's in the hospital." Damian's shoulder bag dropped heavily to the floor, then he sunk down on the other sofa with a sigh and dragged his hands through his hair. "The one he went to the cinema with—he killed himself."

I drew in a sharp breath. Of all the things that could've happened to someone going to watch a film —that hadn't even been close to the top of the list.

"Shit." Silver pushed gently against me and I quickly pulled away from him so he could sit up and be closer to Damian. "Is Josh all right? Have you been to see him?"

Damian shook his head. "Angelina said Josh was all right physically, but they had to sedate him because he wouldn't stop screaming. He's not doing well mentally, and I'm scared for tomorrow."

"Why?"

"Because I don't know what it'll be like when I go to see him. He hasn't been hospitalised since we met, so I don't know how bad it's going to be." He fell into thoughts for a few moments, then he stood up just as quickly as he'd sat down. "I'm going to bed."

Silver bit down on his lip and glanced at me.

I could only press my lips together. I had nothing to say. I didn't know *what* to say.

All I could think about was how difficult a relationship was for Damian and Josh—while for Silver and me, it'd been so very easy from the start.

"Shit." He fell back on the sofa.

"You could say that." I scooted in close to him. "Poor Josh. He was happy about going to the cinema earlier, and now... now everything's gone to shit for him. And his friend... I mean, what could happen at the bloody cinema to lead to such an end to the night?"

He shook his head then simply gazed at me quietly for nearly a minute. "I hate to say it, but I'm glad we've got the relationship we have."

"I was just thinking the same thing." I stroked his arm, feeling the tight biceps. "We've had it easy, haven't we? Besides the whole HIV mess." Which I definitely did *not* like to think about. I'd rather put that whole debacle behind me.

It was definitely the episode that could've made our newfound relationship quite hard, but because Silver was wonderful, it hadn't been a big issue at all.

Silver took my hand in his. "I say we go to bed, too."

There was heat in his gaze, besides the worry he felt for his mates.

I definitely wouldn't mind losing myself in sex for a while. I found myself wishing Damian would have that, too: something to lose himself in, so he didn't have to worry about his boyfriend—but then, sex wasn't his thing.

Good thing it was our thing.

DAMIAN SAT DEJECTEDLY on the sofa when we got up the next morning.

Having the same weekend off from work was definitely a very good thing, since we could sleep in together and spend lots of time in bed before we actually got up to start our day.

"When are you going to go see Josh?" Silver asked him.

"I'm not."

Silver had been on his way into the kitchen, but

now he did a double-take. I leaned against the edge of the sofa. "Why not?"

"He's not doing so well. No one's allowed to see him."

"Shit, mate." Silver went over to put a hand on his shoulder. I saw him squeeze tightly.

"Why don't you come out with us?" I offered. "We're eating lunch, then Silver's going to give Chloe a new tattoo."

Damian didn't look convinced. "I guess I could do lunch, at least."

"Good." Silver squeezed his shoulder again then took a step back. "We'll just get ready, then."

He only nodded. He was dressed, so I suspected he'd already been out, to the hospital to see Josh.

"I hope everything will be okay with them," I said once we were locked in the bathroom.

"Josh is strong. He's been through a lot. I'm sure he'll get through this, too, he just needs time and space and lots of help."

I could only nod, as I'd stuffed my toothbrush in my mouth.

Silver only stared down at his. "It's worse with Damian. He's strong, too, but like, he's not good at asking anyone for help. *And* he's difficult to read, so I'm not sure just how much support to give or if he prefers to be alone."

I spit out the toothpaste. "Well, I'm sure he'll tell you if he needs some alone time," I suggested before resuming brushing.

"Yeah, maybe." He added toothpaste and started brushing his teeth, too.

It was quite a domestic scene: one we didn't experience all that often, as I normally started work before he did. I smiled around the toothbrush.

He met my eyes in the mirror—and after a brief second of staring, he smiled back, too.

"I STILL RECKON we should do a double date."

Chloe pouted at me from where she sat in the black leather chair.

I only stared back, unimpressed. It wasn't that I didn't like going out with her, or that I didn't like Quinn, because I did. I just didn't see the point of a double date. Silver and I didn't really do dates on our own, even, except our very first lunch date after we'd hooked up.

"Silver." Chloe turned her pout to my boyfriend. "Don't you think it's a good idea? Double date? Tell your boyfriend to get that stick out of his arse."

"I haven't got a stick anywhere near my arse."

"Oh, really?" She waggled her eyebrows at me, eyes darting to Silver and back to me again.

Okay, so I'd kind of set myself up for that one.

Silver chuckled, but was still intent on his work on Chloe's upper arm.

She was having the opposite one from where she'd previously had the pin-up woman done. Looking at that design brought back a flush of nice memories for me, and I cast Silver a loving look he didn't see.

"So why more butterflies?" She had butterflies going down the upper part of her spine, from her hairline down to her shoulder blades. Now she was having bigger ones done on her arm—and they were in colour, too.

"Because I like butterflies."

"It doesn't have a deep, meaningful *meaning*?"

"Not at all." She grinned at me. "It doesn't have to have, you know. All that matters is that you like the design." Her grin faded and she looked me up and down. "When're you getting your tattoo?"

I shrugged, my gaze going to Silver's hand working the tattoo-needle. It was still such an erotic sight. I wasn't sure I could contain myself if I had to watch him work on me.

"I haven't figured out what I want yet. It's not like I can draw anything for myself."

"I'll draw you something, babe," Silver said. "Something quite fitting to you, something not like anything I've seen someone else have."

"Aww. Now that deserves at least a kiss."

"If you want your tattoo done, you better not suggest that." It was my turn to waggle my eyebrows at her. "If I start kissing him, I won't be able to stop. And I'm pretty sure you won't want to be here to witness what that leads to."

"Actually, I don't think I would mind. I haven't seen a cock in ages—least of all two. If I can't enjoy it close-up anymore, at least I can enjoy it from a distance."

I burst out laughing, both at her voice and at the surprised expression on Silver's face.

"I thought you were gay?" He tipped the needle away from her skin, allowing him to look up at her inquiringly.

"Nope." She popped the p. "I'm bi. I've actually been with more blokes than girls, but… well, Quinn's great. She stole my heart."

"Now *that's* cliché."

She threw me a dirty look. "Like *he* didn't steal *yours*. Thanks to *me*, I might add."

She had a point.

A very fair, very true point.

"And I am eternally grateful that you let yourself be bribed."

She was taken aback. She glanced at Silver. "You told him about that, huh?"

"I came clean about it before we even hooked up." He tipped his head down, almost sheepishly.

I chuckled. "More like the moment she was out the door." I pointed towards the door, just to properly get the point across.

Now she was the one laughing at us.

Silver threw me a suggestive look. "And I don't regret it for a second. It worked out wonderful for me."

I beamed. I couldn't help it. Compliments from my boyfriend made me happier than anything else.

Silver went back to tattooing, and my eyes were drawn to his movements.

Oh wow, instant boner.

Chloe must've seen how tight my jeans had suddenly become, or she'd seen something on my face, because she laughed at me again.

I didn't care.

I was too busy ogling my boyfriend's hands tattooing her pale skin.

CHAPTER 13

I woke with a start by an elbow jamming into my side.

I rolled over onto my stomach, then dragged a hand through my hair as I propped myself up with my elbows.

Silver was asleep, but it was a restless sleep. His head moved back and forth on the pillow and his arms couldn't lie still. I reached down with one arm to rub against my side where his elbow had rammed into me.

Blimey, that hurt.

I'd probably have a bruise to show for it.

"Silver, love." I touched his shoulder softly.

He sighed in his sleep, and then flipped over to lie on his stomach. His wide back was bared to my eyes and I flicked on the bedside lamp to see it properly. I'd never had an opportunity to study the intricate tattoo without him knowing I was studying it, and I took full advantage of that now.

At the centre of his back, over his shoulder blades, and down his spine, was a cross. An ornate, intricate cross. Fanning out from it was a pair of wings. They took the rest of the space over his shoulder blades and went down his back and sides. The tips curved over his arse. The letters I'd spotted once before, the *R.I.P.*, went over the topmost part of the cross. But now, I saw there were three sets of initials underneath it, too, worked into the design so well that I'd initially thought them to be part of the texture of the cross.

But whose initials were they?

The whole back piece was elaborate. It was also very gloomy, with its dark colours and shadowed greys. Only dark red stood out at certain places, like on the roses wound around the cross.

I also knew what his collarbone tattoo meant now, too.

Memento mori.

It was inked in with the same gothic writing as the initials on his back.

Remember your mortality. Remember you must die.

At first, I'd thought it was just a nice saying, but

coupled with the *R.I.P.* on his back, and now the three initials I hadn't spotted before, I was afraid it had a more sinister meaning.

I turned the light back off and rolled over, so I could be close to him.

He had calmed down, and I lay very close to his side and slid my hand softly over his back in a caress.

Maybe it *was* time to start prying into his life a little, or at least try to.

Silver didn't *have* to share with me, but it would be real nice if he did. That's what relationships were about, right? To share and trust each other. Lean on each other...

I inched even closer, until I was pressed up against his back. I rested my cheek in between his shoulder blades and wrapped my arm around his waist. He was hot against me, but it was nice compared to the chilly temperature of the room.

Silver was always warm and he was always good at warming me up whenever I was cold.

"Love you." I murmured it against the tattooed skin I was pressed up against.

To think that we'd now been together four months.

It was unreal.

It was the best four months of my *life*. They had most certainly been four months of bliss, coupled with a lot of worry about both of his flatmates, whom I'd come to care about so very much as well.

I hoped that Silver wasn't having second thoughts, though. I hoped he didn't ever get tired of me.

Don't think like that.

I'd promised myself after the whole HIV scare that I wouldn't jump to such conclusions without any proof.

Something *was* bothering Silver though, that was obvious.

But I had a feeling it had a lot more to do with his tattoos than with me.

If only I'd known what it was. That way I could've tried to help him or comfort him.

As it was now…

I felt a bit helpless.

WE EMERGED to a made table the next morning.

It was made for five and filled with food. There was milk, juice, water, two different types of bread, eggs, bacon, hash browns, beans… it was quite the breakfast feast.

Sun-Hi smiled at us as she turned from the fridge. "Happy Christmas! You're just in time." She gestured to the table, where both my dad and Kasey were already seated amongst the heap of food she'd prepared.

"Morning," Dad greeted us before going back to his paper.

Kasey glanced up at me and smiled. But when his eyes cut to Silver, he lowered his head again quickly with a blush.

I waggled my eyebrows at Silver teasingly.

He only shook his head and bumped my shoulder, but he smiled, too. He found Kasey's crush cute —and amusing.

Sun-Hi sat down on her seat opposite Dad. "I was wondering if you two could go to the shop later? I forgot to get a couple of things for supper yesterday."

"Of course we can," Silver replied readily as he reached for the milk carton.

"You can take the car." Dad folded his paper and put it aside.

Silver froze up next to me. "I don't drive."

I looked at him oddly.

"Don't you have your licence, son?" Dad asked curiously.

I knew he had his licence, I'd seen the card in his wallet.

So what was this about?

The question of driving had never come up

before. It didn't make any sense to drive a car in the middle of London. It was simpler, not to mention faster, to take the bus or the tube.

"Well, yeah, I do, but… I just don't like to drive."

I put my hand on his arm. "We can walk. It's no big deal. It's not that far."

Sun-Hi looked between us, a slightly confused frown marring her eyebrows.

I shared her confusion wholeheartedly.

"I SHOULD EXPLAIN what that was all about."

I glanced over at him.

He was dressed up in his thick winter jacket and he had his hands buried in his pockets.

I huddled in my own jacket, where I walked briskly next to him. "Does it have something to do with your back tattoo?"

His head turned to me, but he couldn't quite meet my gaze. "It does. You've never asked about my back piece before."

"I've never given it much thought, to be honest. You have so many tattoos. But I looked at it last night when you woke me up and I realised I probably should've paid a lot more attention to it than I have."

He frowned. "I woke you up?"

"Oh, yeah, you kind of—" How to say it without him feeling guilty? My side was still tender. "Well, you jabbed me in the side with your elbow. Seemed like you were having a really bad dream."

"I'm sorry. It's just… it's today."

"What's today?" I was thoroughly confused.

"The anniversary of their deaths." He hunched his shoulders and shuddered. "You've never asked me specifically why I lived with Vincent either, before Damian and I got our flat."

"I figured if you wanted to share the reason with me, you would. I don't really know much about your mum and dad, besides what you've told me here and there. I know you don't come from the same situation I do, but I also know something must've happened. Your whole back's a memorial piece."

He ran one hand through his hair. "I told you I was the surprise child that was never meant to happen. They were older, maybe too lenient with me. I was a handful, too, I can admit that now. I wasn't easy on them."

I knew all this, so I waited silently for him to continue. His parents might be alive and well, but someone close to him had died.

Someone so close to him that he had their initials inked on his back.

Someone important enough to use his whole back as a tribute to them.

"I got my licence when I was seventeen. I was the first in my group of friends to get it. I didn't have my own car, but we wanted to go out for a drive, hit up this party in the next town over, so I took my parents' car without their permission." He hunched his shoulders again.

I could tell this was a painful subject to him. I was pretty sure I knew where it was going, too, but I hoped I was mistaken.

"There were four of us, three blokes and a girl. They were all my best friends. I was in love with one of them, and he liked me back and we had a good thing going. Thing was, our girl friend was in love with *me* and we decided to tell her about us on the drive. She didn't take it well. We started arguing and it was all so bloody pointless, you know?" He dragged both his hands through his hair, pulling slightly.

I winced at the sight.

"The next thing I knew, the car hit a slippery patch and it swerved off the road. It went right over the ditch and hit a tree."

I closed my eyes for a second.

It was going to end the way I'd suspected. Three sets of initials on his back, three friends in the car with him… it wasn't hard to do the math, even for me, who'd done terrible at math in school.

"I woke up in hospital with a sprained wrist, lots of bruises, and a concussion. They told me I was lucky. Then, they told me that my three mates, one of whom was my boyfriend, were dead." He wiped at his face.

Just like living with a mental illness, this was another thing I couldn't fathom what it must be like. How he must've felt.

"I didn't do so well afterwards. Fell off the deep end a little. I didn't go to college, so I failed the entire year. My parents… they didn't know what to do with me, so when they decided to send me to live with Vincent in London, I was all for it. I didn't want to stay there anymore, with everything that had happened." He gazed off ahead. "Vincent did better with me. He got through to me with all that psycho-analyses stuff he's so bloody good at. I refused to see a psychologist, but as Vincent is one, I suppose that's what I did anyway. Doesn't really matter though. He helped me a lot. I got my head back on straight and retook the last year of college so I could get my A-levels."

I stepped closer, so our arms were pressed together. I hoped it was of some comfort to him. "I'm so sorry, love."

"I know I'm not to blame, not entirely." He flashed me a small, barely-there smile. "It took Vince a while to get that through my head. It wasn't my fault that the road was slippery, it wasn't my fault that she reacted the way she did, that the entire argument got out of hand. That it could've happened just as easily if my entire focus had been on the road." He sighed and tilted his head back, staring skywards. "I'm never going to forget them or the accident. I'm never going to *not* blame myself. I know some of the blame is on me, I do, but not all of it."

I looped one arm around his elbow and held on to him as he kept talking, his voice strained.

"I drew my back piece as a memorial to them. As a way to show that I'd never forget. As a way to show how much I cared about them all, despite what happened that night. I know she was hurt and that she reacted from that hurt and that, given time, she would've accepted it. She was always an act first, think later kind of girl." He smiled bitterly. "I had the tattoo done at the shop, actually. I went there to get it done, got talking with the boss, and with a bright and shiny A* in Arts, I got a trainee position with him. It all worked out brilliantly for me."

I hugged him close.

We were nearing the shop now, but our steps had slowed considerably as he talked.

"I hate the fact they died, but at the same time, I'm grateful that I'm still alive. I started taking one day at a time, to not worry about the future and just live my life. That's what they would've wanted. They wouldn't have wanted me to beat myself up over it for the rest of my life. Usually, I manage quite well and I thought *this* year won't be so bad, but then Christmas rolled around and it all came washing up on me again and I just feel so *bad*." He hugged me close as well now. "I'm sorry my bad dreams woke you up last night. I'm sorry I hurt you."

"It's okay, babe. I don't mind the occasional jab in the side, as long as I can be there for you whenever you need me." All I wanted was to be with him. We'd only been together four months, but that was enough to know what I wanted. And I wanted a life with him in it.

He stopped, forcing me to a halt also, and turned so he could cup his free hand over my cheek. His palm was warm from having been shoved in his pocket and I revelled in the feel against my own cold cheek. "You being there helps a tremendous lot." He bent and brushed a chaste kiss over my lips.

Nothing could warm me more than hearing those words.

CHAPTER 14

"*H*ere's my gift."

I handed over the finely-wrapped present as I anxiously chewed on my bottom lip.

Silver unwrapped it slowly—almost too slow, *torturously* slow.

Once the paper I'd spent an hour on getting just right was off, Silver turned the book over in his hands a couple of times, presumably to take in the ruby-coloured cover.

Two simple words were written on the front in elegant, gold writing.

Our memories.

Silver flipped the book open to reveal the first

page. The pages were thick and black, a perfect match for the deep red of the cover. I'd written on the first page in a gold marker.

Silver,

This is to show you how much I've enjoyed our months together. I hope there'll be many more months to come.

Happy Christmas!

I love you.

Kian.

Silver's name was accentuated with a heart after it, while mine was signed with a big heart in front of it. Anxiety curled low in my stomach as I watched his face.

A small smile spread on his lips as he read the first page, then he flipped it over to the first double page. I'd dedicated each double-page to every month we'd been together. I'd pasted in pictures and other stuff that meant something to me, for instance, the ticket to the first film Silver had taken me to.

I'd also written short, sweet sentiments.

Doing a scrapbook like this was romantic and cliché, but I hadn't been able to help myself.

I'd spent such a long time getting the four first double pages just perfect.

Silver flipped over to the second set of double pages.

The first thing that jumped out at me was the picture of the two of us. He was sitting in a chair at the salon, while I was bent down slightly so that our heads were on the same level, and we both smiled into the camera.

Chloe had taken the picture after the first time I'd cut Silver's hair.

He flipped the pages over again.

On the third set of double pages was a picture of a sleeping Silver I'd taken one particular sunny morning. He looked gorgeous lying on his back, with his head turned away from the window and his naked, toned, and tattooed chest at display.

On the fourth set of double pages was a picture of me. We'd been out walking in Hyde Park after work one day and Silver had snapped a picture of me resting on a bench. I smiled widely into the camera and held my hands together in a heart-shaped form.

I'd written with gold marker underneath it.

I love you!

It was accentuated with no less than three hearts.

I felt a flush rise in my cheeks and I bowed my

head as Silver flipped back to look over all the pages again.

"Kian, this is…" He seemed to be lost for words.

I hoped it was a good sort of speechless.

"This is brilliant!" He bent over and enveloped me in a tight, one-armed hug. "I love you, too, you know."

"You don't think it's too cheesy?" I couldn't help feeling embarrassed. I *was* proud of the scrapbook, but it was embarrassing to show it off.

"I think it's just perfect." Silver kissed my cheek and drew back. His fingers slid over a picture of the two of us out to dinner.

"There's another page." I pointed to the book. "I kind of made a head-start on January."

Silver flipped it. His smile faltered and he blinked down at the single picture pasted in the corner of the first page. It was the picture of a drawing. It was something he'd drawn for me.

The original was a big one he'd drawn in his A3 sketchbook, so it hadn't fit in the scrapbook. It was a drawing of a peacock, with its tail flowing upwards behind it. It was a colourful drawing and not exactly masculine, but then, I'd never been accused of being a masculine bloke.

"This is what you are to me," Silver had said, when he'd drawn it only a couple weeks ago. *"You're beau-*

tiful and colourful and even when I'm having the worst kind of day, you brighten it up simply with your presence."

I'd used the gold marker to draw a frame around the smaller replica of his drawing. Next to it, I'd written something and underlined it elegantly.

The finished tattoo.

Silver lifted his head to look at me. "What's this?"

I smiled slightly and pointed to the picture. "That's going to be my tattoo."

"You want me to tattoo you?" He ran his hand over first the picture, then the writing. "You want *this* as your tattoo?"

"You did say you'd draw me something extraordinary." It hadn't been his exact words, but I was paraphrasing. "*This* is that extraordinary piece. This is something I've never seen anyone else have, and I want it on my body. It's gorgeous and it's perfect and my body is now your canvas."

He turned his head so our lips met. "You know I'm still just a trainee, right? You still want me to do this? It's a big piece of ink."

I grinned against his lips. "I wouldn't want anyone else to do it. You're it, love."

He smiled, too, as he tugged me in close. "I better be."

~

IF BREAKFAST the day before hadn't been a feast, Christmas dinner certainly was. I'd never seen so much food on the table; there was so much that we hardly had space for our plates.

Dad ended up at the head of the table, with Sun-Hi and Kasey on one side, and me and Silver on the other. Silver sat opposite Kasey, and my brother had his head down so low that his forehead almost connected with the table.

It was cute and hilarious, but I also felt sorry for him.

I remembered being young, barely a teenager, and having my first crush on some bloke in my class at the time. It had felt like the most important thing in my life at the time. I'd changed between staring, drooling, and blushing so much that I'd been afraid my face would turn permanently red.

"How's school going, Kasey?" I asked, hoping to distract him a little bit.

He shrugged his thin shoulders. "It's okay." He lifted his head to smile at me, but his eyes instantly cut to Silver, and just like that, he bowed his head again.

Sun-Hi's face split into a smile and I could tell she had difficulty holding back laughter. "It's more than okay. You're doing excellent." She clapped him lightly on the shoulder.

I would've sworn that he couldn't blush more, but I was pretty sure he did.

Dad had started to pile food on his plate, so both Silver and I followed his lead.

Sun-Hi waited until our plates were filled up before she fixed up for herself and Kasey.

"This looks really good," Silver told her, smiling widely.

She beamed happily. "I hope it tastes the same. I won't be offended if you don't like my Korean dishes, though. Not everyone does."

I had no idea what those dishes were, and they looked kind of funny, but I added some on my plate just to get a taste of it.

Silver had already started in on the food, and he complimented her again, causing her to beam wider.

Dinner passed by.

Kasey didn't speak another word, but the rest of us kept the conversation going. Dad and Silver had a long conversation about his work as a tattoo artist. I was proud for my boyfriend, and happy that my dad seemed to be so interested in him.

"He's going to tattoo me soon," I told them.

Dad looked at me. "You know what you're having?"

"Something special he drew just for me." I put my hand on Silver's thigh under the table, squeezing affectionately.

He grinned back. "Very special."

"Your own tattoos are quite impressive." Sun-Hi's gaze dropped to Silver's exposed forearms, both of which were covered in ink. "I hear tattoo artists have to tattoo themselves sometimes. Have you done something on yourself?"

"I have, but not big ones. My boss has done most of them. My entire back and the ones on my chest, as well as most of my sleeves."

Both Dad and Sun-Hi seemed surprised. They'd seen his arms, and I believe his collarbone one morning he'd only been wearing a vest, but they hadn't seen his back. His very impressive back piece.

Conversation moved on from tattoos as we all ate until we were full.

It was, hands down, the nicest dinner I'd ever had.

I'd never celebrated Christmas before. Mum hadn't given a shit about it, so I'd usually spent the day and night either locked up in my room or out at a party or a club.

Dad coming back into my life, and letting me into his family, was the best thing that could've happened to me. I finally had a normal family, instead of a mother who whored around and didn't give a shit as to whether I lived or died. A mother who'd kept my wonderful dad away for all my life.

It was a good thing I'd never known what I'd been missing, or else I wouldn't have been able to quell the bitterness I would've felt over the crappy life she'd given me, just out of spite to him.

As it was, I'd survived, hadn't known what things *could* be like, and everything had been simply *okay*.

Later that night, once Kasey was parked on the sofa with a cartoon on the telly, Dad brought out the beer for him and Silver, while Sun-Hi mixed some kind of drink for me and her.

Dad clinked his bottle with my glass. "I am thankful for you allowing me into your life." His gaze was intense, but sincere.

I swallowed the lump that threatened to get stuck in my throat.

Sun-Hi followed Dad's lead and clinked her glass to mine. "I'm thankful that I got to know you, Kian. That you accepted both me and Kasey, as well as your dad. We've all grown to love you so much. I feel like I've gained a second son."

And cue the waterworks.

I couldn't stop the bloody tears if I'd managed to try; they appeared that fast.

"I didn't mean to make you cry." Sun-Hi leaned in and wiped the back of her hand over one of my cheeks.

"I love you, too," I managed to force out through the big fat lump that was back and stuck. "I am so glad Dad came to get me that day. That you were all willing to get to know me. That you let me *live* here with you while I finished college. I love you *so* much."

Silver's arm snaked over my upper back.

I leaned into him, hiding my face against his neck. I hated crying, most of all because it made me look all red and blotchy, and because it ruined my make-up. I'm sure the eyeliner had made black tracks down my cheeks already.

"We love you, too, so much. Kasey loves having a big brother. He's always been on us to get a little brother, but I think he thinks having an older one is way cooler." Sun-Hi patted my back.

That brought on laughter through my tears and I made some weird noises I didn't even want to think about.

Silver chuckled in my ear and rubbed at my shoulder.

"You know what I'm grateful for?" He said it in a low voice, but not such a low voice that the others wouldn't hear. "I'm grateful to Chloe for letting me bribe her."

I pulled back so I could look up at him. I briefly caught the confused expressions on Dad's and Sun-Hi's faces, but that was to be expected. I hadn't told them *how* I'd met Silver, after all.

"And I am very grateful to Chloe too, for letting herself be bribed." I leaned in and kissed him. I hadn't done that before in front of them, but I was so happy, everything was so good, that I couldn't help myself. He was my boyfriend, they were my family, and they all liked each other.

I couldn't ask for more.

CHAPTER 15

"*H*ey, D, come look at what Kian got me for Christmas."

Damian emerged from his bedroom, which he'd just entered to be rid of his shoulder-bag. He walked slowly, though, seemed to be a bit on edge, as if he wasn't sure he wanted to know.

Silver held out the ruby-coloured book. He seemed happy and proud and excited all at once. It made my stomach squeeze with this wonderful feeling called *love*.

"He got you a journal?"

I chuckled.

"Uh, no." Silver rolled it eyes, pushing it further towards Damian, who finally took it.

He glanced at both of us as if to make sure we

really did want him to look at it, then he started flip-
ping through it.

I held my breath as he flipped through the few
pages that were filled up. This was Silver's best
mate... I wanted for him to approve of the gift I'd
given Silver.

He finally looked up, eyes and face unreadable.
"This was quite... cheesy." He handed the book back
to Silver, and now, my stomach tightened from a
different feeling altogether.

He doesn't like it.

"But sweet. And nicely made."

And the ball of disappointment dissolved. It
wasn't the best compliment, but Damian wasn't very
good at them, and I knew this was the best I'd ever
get from him. I took it and clung to it with my *life*.

"Maybe it gives you some ideas." Silver put the
book down on the table.

"I think not," he snorted. "That's not exactly my
style."

"Doesn't hurt to be a bit romantic, you know."
Silver stretched his arms out over the back of
the sofa.

A troubled expression passed over Damian's face
for a moment. "I'm taking a shower." And just like
that, he'd gone and locked himself in the bathroom.

I looked at Silver.

Silver stared down at his wristwatch.

"What?"

"He's home early from work," was all he said, casting a confused look at the bathroom door.

"Maybe he just wanted some time off." I tipped over to rest my head on his shoulder. "He's so busy with school, and he works, too, and I can't fathom how he makes both, considering just how much studying he has to do."

"He's super smart." Silver's arm, the one that had rested along the back of the sofa, settled around my shoulders. "Hey, Ki, if you want to go home I'll understand."

"What? Why would I want that?"

He looked down at me all understanding. "You haven't been there in two weeks. You haven't seen Chloe in two weeks. Maybe I should show her the book?"

I chuckled. "That book's not such a big deal, you know. Besides, Chloe already knows about it. Where do you think I made it? I had everything spread out on our coffee table."

He tipped his head to one side. "I see your point. Still, if you want to go meet your best mate for a while, I won't mind."

I threw him a shrewd look. "You trying to be rid of me?"

"Never." He kissed my temple.

"You know what I want to do?"

"No. What?"

"We've been staying with my parents, which meant the bedroom next to theirs and no sex. I am ready for some wild shagging right about now."

He threw his head back on a laugh and I leaned in to lick his Adam's apple. It was totally impulsive—but I couldn't help myself.

"Damian's home. It can't be that wild," he cautioned.

"Hey, as long as it involved my arse and your cock, I'm not fussy about the rest of the details."

His grey eyes darkened at my words.

We stared at each other silently for one moment—two—then he dragged me with him into his bedroom and firmly shut the door.

Oh, yeah, the shagging's on.

"BLIMEY!"

I stretched my legs out before standing up from the leather-bound chair I'd been sitting on for the last couple of hours. "It bloody hurts to get a tattoo, but not so much I won't want to do it again."

Silver chuckled behind me. "You're done now."

I strode over to the full-body mirror at the back of the shop and whirled around, so I was standing with my back to it. I craned my neck for a good view of my brand-new ink.

All down my left side was the peacock tattoo he'd drawn for me: the one I'd decided was going to be my very first tattoo. Its tail fanned out over my shoulder blades, out towards my spine, and down my back, and it ended with the peacock's wings and head over the lower part of my back and bum, where it curled slightly over my left arse cheek.

My skin was red and sore, and the tattoo itself was shiny after the ointment he'd slathered all over it. He'd only done the outlining and some shadowing, as the colouring would have to wait, but it still looked truly amazing.

It looked a lot better on my body than on a piece of paper.

"Like it?" Silver came over to me and peered in the mirror as well. A smile curved his lips. I knew he was satisfied with his work.

"I *love* it." I enunciated the *love*, simply because it was *that* amazing and it needed to be vocalised.

"Stand like that for a sec." He disappeared further into the shop, then came back holding a camera. "Better take that picture for the scrap book now, before the skin starts to peel."

I couldn't suppress my grin as I posed for the photo. I'd never thought life would ever be as good as it was now. I'd never thought I'd ever be so content.

But here I was, having soon been with him for five months, and we were still going strong.

And tattooing... I could see why he liked it so much. Seeing your body adorned with such beautiful designs was a feeling like nothing else. A feeling that told me that there'd be a lot more tattooing in my future.

More tattoos and more Silver.

I didn't mind. Not at all.

"Proposing we do this tonight was an *excellent* idea." We'd been lounging in bed, after some hot sex, and he'd suggested we head down to the shop to get started on the tattoo.

I'd jumped out of bed in excitement.

And now, here we were, with the outline of it expertly done. I couldn't be happier.

"Come here, I'll wrap it up for you." Silver motioned me back towards the chair, and I sat down, so he could put clean film over the entire tattoo, making it hold with tape.

I wasn't exactly looking forward to taking the tape off, but I suppose it was a necessary precaution.

He handed me my shirt once he was done and I

gingerly shimmied into it, being very careful about my left side.

Silver cleaned up and put everything away, while I sat silently on the chair and watched him. I loved the way his muscles moved and how his shirt stretched tight over his broad shoulders.

"You are the most handsome bloke I've ever seen."

He barked out a laugh. "Where did that come from?" He shrugged on his jacket and came over to me, holding his hand out for me to take.

I entwined our fingers as we made our way out of the shop. "It's simple truth."

He locked the shop up, pocketed his keys again, and then we headed towards home. Or his home, anyway. It wasn't exactly mine. Though, I did spend more time there lately than I did in my own flat.

His Christmas present to me had been a key to said flat, so I could come and go whenever I wanted, without having to wait for him or schedule with him.

It had been a wonderful surprise to get that key—but I wasn't complaining at all. It definitely meant he was as serious as I was.

When we walked in the door, we were met with a surprise.

We were met by Damian sitting on the sofa—with Josh next to him.

I hadn't seen Josh since the end of November, and he didn't look at all different from what he had back then, but there was still something about him. He seemed happier, perhaps.

"Josh!" I hugged him quite impulsively.

We'd never done that before, but he'd been gone for so long and it felt right. I wasn't sure what Damian felt about me hugging his boyfriend, but he didn't seem to mind it when I chanced a quick glance over at him.

"It's so good to see you again." I stroked his cheek once I drew back. I didn't know why I did it. Maybe I just wanted to show him some affection, or just make sure it was actually him, that he was really out of hospital.

Once I stepped back, Silver took my place. He hugged Josh hard and for even longer, but then, he was closer to him than I was. He'd dealt with him a *lot* more than I had.

Damian watched the two of them wryly, and I swear there was a small smile tilting the corner of his lips up.

I had no idea what had happened in the time span of Damian coming home early from work to Silver tattooing me, but Josh was back and they both seemed happy. Really, that was all that mattered, wasn't it?

Now that Josh was back here with Damian, and I was still here with Silver, everything felt right again. Chloe might be my best friend and flatmate, but I felt at home with Silver and *his* flatmates.

"You lads hungry?" Silver stepped back, standing at my side, and he looked at all three of us. "How about we order some take-away and just spend the evening on the sofa?"

I was all in for that, and Damian and Josh seemed to be as well.

"How are you?" I sat down on the sofa while Silver called to order the food.

Josh curled up on himself, but he smiled slightly. He cast a quick glance at Damian, then focused on me. "I'm better. I'm not *fine*, but I'm better. And that feels good."

After everything I'd heard about borderline, I guess feeling better or good must be extraordinary. I didn't doubt for a second that Damian had a big part in it. He'd been crushed when Josh had been admitted to hospital at the end of November, but he'd been to see him often, and now here they were together again. They seemed happy.

Silver dropped down beside me once he'd finished on the phone. His arm stretched over my shoulder, pulling me in tight to him.

"Oh, hey, babe." He looked at me, a bit startled.

"What?" I stared back, not understanding.

"You have to take off the clean film and wash the tattoo."

"Oh! Right." Now that he mentioned it, I could feel the uncomfortable clean film on my back. And the thought of ripping of the tape made me shudder.

"You got a tattoo?" Josh leaned forward a bit, looking at me with interest.

"Want to see it?" I grinned, proud of my new, and first, piece of ink.

Josh nodded eagerly and I jumped to my feet.

Damian's eyes were on me as well now.

I pulled my shirt over my head, quickly, and whirled around so they'd see my back.

"It's not done. It's going to be in colour, but that would be too much work for one day." I craned my neck, but without a mirror, I couldn't see it. I could see some of the outline on my shoulder, but that was it.

"Let me help you take it off." Silver was next me and he ripped the first tape off without a warning.

I squealed indignantly, and then steeled myself for the other ones. I had to grit my teeth so hard I felt it in my jaw, but at least the tape was gone.

He took the clean film off and balled it up in his hand.

"That is stunning."

I craned my head the other way to grin at Josh. "I know, right? My boyfriend is amazing."

"Indeed he is." Josh nodded in agreement.

I turned around to face them head on, eyes going to Damian. He'd been looking at my tattoo, I could tell, but once he was faced with my bare chest, his head turned away.

I couldn't stop a giggle escaping.

He was so prudish when it came to sex or nakedness that it was funny.

The one time he'd walked in on Silver and I in a *very* compromising position—naked and shagging, as it were—it seemed like he was *this close* to passing out. His face had been beet-red.

"Just a chest." I motioned down it for emphasis. "Nothing wrong to look at it."

Josh laughed, but Damian didn't seem as amused.

Silver chuckled then put me in a headlock. "Come on, funny guy, time to wash that up and put ointment on it."

I followed him into the bathroom, where he proceeded to do everything. It wasn't like I could do it myself, after all. My arms weren't that limber.

Once he'd rubbed ointment all over the tattoo, he disappeared for a minute without a word, leaving me standing there confused.

Then he came back and handed me a loose vest.

I pulled it on gingerly, being careful, so that it wouldn't stick too much to the ointment.

It was my vest, so it fit me. If it'd been one of his, my entire chest would've still been on display. But I had my own drawer in his room—had it for a while—and it seemed to fill up more and more each week.

When we walked back out into the living room, Damian and Josh were leaning in close to each other, having a whispered conversation.

There was a small smile on Josh's lips and his eyes seemed to light up.

It was so nice to see him happy.

The doorbell rang, and Silver headed out to get our food.

"Were we in the bathroom *that* long?" I ventured into the kitchen to get cutlery and glasses and two different bottles of soft drinks, since I didn't know what they'd prefer.

Silver was already back with the food by the time I ventured out into the living room. Josh and Damian both leaned forward to help sort the different Chinese take-away, while I handed out the glasses and cutlery.

"This is nice," Silver said when we'd all finally started eating.

"What'd you mean?" Damian arched an eyebrow at him.

Silver grinned. "The four of us, together again, enjoying our evening. I don't know about you, but I think it's nice."

"It is," Josh agreed. "I've missed this the past month. I've missed all of you so much." He rested his head against Damian's shoulder, seemingly to fight off some emotion.

Damian put a hand on his knee in return and I saw him squeeze the tiniest bit.

It was the most intimate thing I'd caught them in. That simple show of affection. Damian wasn't a very affectionate person, at least not in public. I had no idea what he was like when it was just the two of them. It was cute, though.

I turned to Silver. He smiled at me.

"I love you *so* much," I whispered.

He put his take-away box on the table, and cupped his hand at the back of my neck, drawing me in close. "Love you, too. Very much—a lot, even."

I snorted, but then he kissed me, and all thoughts of laughter were blown away. My own box of Chinese food stood in great danger of being tipped over, but I clutched it to my chest as he continued kissing me—and I answered the kiss in turn.

He still grinned when he pulled back. "I'm so glad I took a chance, and that it worked out like this."

"I'm glad you did too." I couldn't imagine how the last four months would've been without him. What would I be doing if he hadn't bribed Chloe to bring me, if I hadn't fallen instantly in lust with him?

I owed Chloe for the rest of my *life*.

But that was more than okay, because she'd brought me to the best thing *in* my life. I'd owe her anything for that.

EPILOGUE

ONE YEAR LATER

Spending Christmas with Silver's parents had been something new and exciting—until they opened the door all smiles to find both their children, and how both smiles instantly fell when they saw me.

"Your parents hate me. No, scratch that. They *loathe* me."

Silver sat down next to my hunched form on the sofa. "They don't loathe you, love. They just don't understand you. They're old and set in their ways and you're..." He motioned to me as a whole. "You're a bit out there. They don't understand me, either, with all the tattoos and stuff."

I looked up at him from underneath my fringe. "I've never been greeted so coolly in my life before, except from my mum. And she's a right bitch. They're *your* parents. They have to love *you*. But not me."

"Babe." Silver slid one muscular arm over my thin shoulders. "They'll warm up to you. It's Christmas. Mum loves Christmas. It always puts her in a good mood. Besides, Vincent's here as well. She's always happy when he comes to visit."

I rubbed a hand over my face and sighed. "I don't want to change who I am. Not for anyone. But I still want them to like me, and all they do is think I'm ridiculous."

"I don't care what they think about you, love." Silver squeezed my shoulders tight. "I like you, Kian, no matter what they have to say about it. Next Christmas, we'll stay back in London. I'm not exactly thrilled about being back, either. Vincent's the favourite, after all."

Last Christmas, our first together, had been wonderful. We'd celebrated with my family: my dad, step-mum, and my little brother. It had been so nice and cosy.

I had no hope this Christmas would be a repeat, though.

"Let's go for a walk." Silver stood up and pulled me to his feet as well. "We can both use some fresh air."

We could certainly use an escape from that house.

We'd only been here for a few hours, but I was already exhausted.

So we bundled up in our thick winter clothes and went outside. I wasn't familiar with the small town, so I let Silver lead the way. We walked in silence.

When I spotted a graveyard ahead, I knew something was up, and I looked over at Silver.

He stared at the ground in front of him, so he didn't notice.

Silently, we passed the open gates.

I had a feeling I knew exactly where we were going. I both dreaded it and felt a morbid sense of curiosity at the same time.

"So this is him." Silver stopped in front of a big, black gravestone engraved with gold writing. "My boyfriend. Ex-boyfriend, I mean." He scratched at his forehead, eyes squeezed closed.

I didn't mind the slip too terribly. They'd never broken up, so this bloke wasn't exactly an ex. He'd been Silver's boyfriend till the last second.

I took in the gold lettering: name, dates, and a line about how much he would be missed. If he'd survived the accident, Silver never would've left town, never would've met me.

For the life of me, I couldn't feel sorry about the fact he was dead, because Silver was the most important person in my life. I couldn't even imagine being without him.

But I could feel sorry about the grief Silver had suffered upon finding out he was dead—and his two friends besides him.

What would my life have been like if I hadn't met Silver? Would I still be sleeping around? Trying to find something that would feel right, that would feel real? It was a likely possibility.

I slid my hands into Silver's, twining our fingers, then wondered if maybe it was inappropriate to do so in front of his previous boyfriend's grave.

But Silver squeezed my hand in return, so apparently it was an okay gesture.

I didn't say anything, since this must be difficult for him: bringing the new boyfriend to meet the dead one.

This was a person Silver had loved.

He might've been young, not even eighteen, but that didn't mean Silver hadn't loved him any less.

After a while, Silver brought me further down the graveyard, and once again, he stopped in front of a gravestone. This was a stone made out of smooth, white marble, and, to judge from the name, this was the girl friend.

Once again, Silver stood in silence, just staring

down at the grave, and I stood quietly by his side, not wanting to interrupt.

I wondered what it must've felt like to wake up in hospital and find out your three closest friends were dead—after the car *he'd* been driving had skittered off the road. I couldn't even imagine it, because I'd never experienced anything even close to it.

Same pattern repeated itself in front of the third gravestone.

Utter silence.

When we left the graveyard again, with another stop in at the first grave, Silver let out a low, not-at-all-happy laugh. "I wish we could leave. Go back to London and forget about this place."

"We can if you want." I was more than eager to leave, but not for the same reasons as he.

I didn't feel threatened by the people whose gravestones we'd just visited. They were a part of Silver's past. A past he'd never forget about, but past nonetheless.

No, I wanted to get away from the parents, who hadn't said a word to me besides the initial chilly hello.

He blinked over at me, like he was surprised I was even there for a moment. "I'm sorry about this."

"About what?"

"Bringing you here and then not saying a word."

Our hands were still linked.

An elderly couple walking by cast us a long look, but it was of no matter. I could hold hands with my boyfriend if I wanted to without worrying about other people's reactions.

If they didn't like it, they were free to look the other way.

"This is your personal pain. I'm just happy you chose to bring me along with you. I hope I was of some comfort." I stepped in closer, so the rest of our arms were in contact now, too.

"You were." He squeezed my hand tight. "You're great, you know that?"

"Well, I try. Sometimes I don't even have to try at all."

His hand slipped from mine and suddenly he had me in a chokehold. "Cheeky little shit, aren't you?"

I laughed as I tried to break free. As long as he was set on keeping me like that, though, I didn't stand a chance. "Got you in a better mood, didn't I?"

He eased the hold, but grabbed my waist and spun me around. I found myself pressed up against his front—and then his lips were on mine, kissing me with a passion I hadn't expected so close to the graveyard that held his worst memories.

"I love you so much," he said once he pulled back.

I drew in a deep breath.

That kiss had caught me completely off-guard—but it had been a *good* caught-off-guard.

"I love you, too." I jabbed my finger against his thick jacket, which was thick enough that he probably didn't even feel it. "And you know it."

"I do." He wrapped one arm around my shoulder as we headed back to his parents' house.

With each step we took, I felt dread curl in my stomach.

"You really want to leave?"

"If the rest of Christmas is going to be like the past couple of hours, then yeah." It was better to be honest. I didn't want to lie and make myself miserable—and he wouldn't appreciate me sugar-coating it, either.

"We'll give it a couple of days, and if they haven't changed their attitude by then, we'll leave."

"You can stay if you want," I offered, though I definitely didn't want him to if I left. "It's your family."

"They are. But I'm not so attached that I have to stay with them for Christmas. Besides, you're my family now, too." His ice-cold fingers brushed the back of my neck and I shivered.

I liked the sound of that.

We'd been together for a year and four months

now. It was the longest relationship I'd ever been in—

Okay, so it was the only relationship I'd been in.

But it was a long time.

It was long enough to know that I wanted the past one year to turn into two, three, a decade. I couldn't get enough of him. He was on my mind every single day when we weren't together, and when we were, I couldn't keep my hands to myself.

I was happy—and it was wonderful.

Vincent was outside when we got back. He was leaning against the wall next to the front door, having a fag.

"Still smoking, are you?" Silver commented drily.

"Oh, come on. I don't smoke that often."

It was true. I hadn't found out Vincent was a smoker until months after we'd met. He wasn't one of those who needed a smoke every hour. He smoked whenever the craving hit him, and it wasn't all that often. I was pretty sure he could have a pack for over a week, maybe even two.

"Why are you smoking now?" Silver eyed him.

"Because I'm stressed." His eyes fell on me. "I had a chat with them about you. Told them to get their act together, as we *do* live in the modern world. And I told them just how good you are for my little brother."

His words warmed me.

"Really?" Butterflies fluttered around in my stomach.

"Did they loosen up?" Silver's arm around my shoulder tightened.

Vincent blew out some smoke. "They haven't yet. I'm sorry." The last part was directed at me.

My stomach instantly knotted back into a ball of dread.

Silver led me back inside.

"That doesn't sound promising," I muttered.

And it really wasn't.

Dinner was tense. Hardly anyone spoke, and I kept my head down and ate everything on my plate.

We all went to bed silently.

Silver tried to lift my mood, but how could it be lifted when his parents *hated* me?

When I woke the next morning, Silver was already up and gone. I dressed, made myself presentable, then went looking for him.

"He looks like a *girl*, Sylvester," I heard Silver's mother's voice coming from the kitchen. "If you want someone who looks like a girl, why don't you just find yourself a real one?"

I stopped dead in my tracks.

"Mum, I'm gay." Silver's voice was exasperated.

"Why don't you find yourself a real man then?"

"He *is* a real man. Just because he isn't all buff and macho doesn't make him any less. So what if he wears make-up? What does it matter if he works as a hairdresser and constantly dyes his hair? That's nothing to you, is it? I'm happy. That should be enough."

"I just don't get it."

"Apparently not."

I blew out a breath. It bothered me that they didn't approve of me, of course it did. They *were* Silver's parents.

But at the same time, I was damned if I was going to change for them.

That wasn't going to happen in, like, *ever*. I was happy with who I was, and nothing was going to change that.

And the people who mattered the most—Silver and my family—didn't mind it. They loved me for who I was.

I took a deep breath, did a mental brush-down, then strode into the kitchen.

They weren't going to intimidate me into not being *me*.

"Morning, babe." I leaned up and placed a kiss directly on his lips, with a louder smack than usual, just for the heck of it.

I might be upset, but that didn't stop me from

being defiant. If they already didn't like me, it didn't matter if it got *worse*. I had nothing to lose, and I was going to treat my boyfriend the same as I always did.

"You've got tattoos," she said, after turning away from the both of us.

"I do." I looked down on my arms. Down one arm were butterflies in various colours, and on the inside of the forearm on the other, I had an intricate pair of scissors, as a homage to my chosen profession.

The butterflies were because they were pretty, and I wanted a sleeve with butterflies and flowers and rainbows and happy things—much like Chloe, though she stuck to only butterflies.

Only the butterflies had been inked on my skin so far, but it was a work in progress. "Your son is very talented."

"He's done them all?" She turned now, a flicker of interest on her wrinkled face.

"I wouldn't have anyone else ink something onto my skin. I'm his canvas." I smiled lovingly up at Silver. "Want to see the biggest piece he's done?" I turned my back on her and wrung my T-shirt up, showing off the big, magnificent peacock, which had been the very first tattoo he'd given me.

"You did that?" She sounded surprised, which...

really? Hadn't she ever seen her son draw? Or seen the skill he possessed with a tattoo needle?

"I did, yeah." Silver grinned. "That's the first thing I ever did on him. Back in January, right after last Christmas."

"It's beautiful." She still sounded shocked.

I let my tee fall back down and turned back around. She blinked once she was faced with my front again, and I was once again reminded that she *did not approve* of the way I looked.

However, I think there was a small smile when she turned away. Maybe we'd broken the ice just a little bit.

~

"You sure it's okay that we'll be out for the evening?"

Silver's mum fussed with her purse, while her husband stood patiently out on the porch waiting for her.

"Yeah, yeah. Go out and enjoy an evening with your mates." Silver all but shooed her out the door. "Have some drinks with your food, have loads of fun. Don't even dare come back before midnight!"

She clapped his cheek in a motherly fashion. "You enjoy your evening, too."

"I will." He grinned widely, which to me held loads of promise, but which she didn't seem to pick up on at all.

"You'll have the telly all to yourself. No more football for tonight." She tottered down the stairs, completely oblivious to the fact that the last thing we were going to do while alone was watch the *telly*.

Silver closed and locked the door once their car drove off, then he turned to me with a smouldering look. "Ready?"

"I was born ready." I jumped on him, and his hands grabbed my arse to keep me lifted while he ascended the stairs.

He kicked the door to his room open, then closed, before depositing me on the bed.

Clothes were thrown around haphazardly as we got rid of them, and finally, we were both pressed together naked on the bed, hard and aching.

I'd come expecting to be celibate for the entirety of Christmas.

After all, it wouldn't be the best impression to have sex in his parents' house while they slept down the hall. But with them out for a few hours and Vincent gone with some of his old mates, too... We took the opportunity presented and *ran* with it.

Or shagged, as it was.

Condoms were a thing of the past, and when my

ankles rested on his shoulders, he pressed into me bare. Having sex bare was... I didn't have words for what it was.

It was *amazing*: the pleasure so raw and so intense. Wearing condoms was nothing at all like this —and I was never going back to being fucked with one again, at least not if I stayed with Silver.

Which I hoped I did.

He leaned over, bracing his arms on the bed on either side of me. The position bent me over almost in half, but it was one of our favourites.

I'd got a lot more limber after I started seeing Silver than I'd ever been before. Being folded over like this was no painful stretch. It only served to intensify the pleasure as he thrust into me, hitting that sweet spot head on with every single thrust.

I tried to keep my moaning to a minimum, just in case anyone did come home, but eventually, I lost all inhibitions.

Who wouldn't, with this man doing his thing?

He knew my body better than I did by now, and I knew his. We could get each other off in a minute or draw it out for several.

Now he was drawing it out, his thrusts deep, but slow, not quite enough force in them to bring me over the edge, but enough to make me vibrate with pleasure.

"You're so gorgeous, love."

I opened my eyes—when had I closed them?—to peer up at him.

He was intent on the task, drops of sweat gathering on his forehead.

"Get me off," I begged. "Please."

He changed rhythm, driving into me now with enough force to rock both me and the bed. It was enough. With a few strokes of his hand on my cock, I came, spurting onto my own chest and over his fingers.

"Yeah, yeah, yeah," I chanted, spine bowing and head tilting back.

"Fucking gorgeous." He bent his head to suck on my neck, intensifying my pleasure.

I was reduced to incoherent moaning.

He kept on thrusting even after I was milked dry and the pleasure was almost intolerable by now.

He was close.

I could tell by the way his thrusts changed back to slower and deeper.

The slow trickle of semen down my skin barely preceded his collapsing atop me.

I wrapped both arms and legs around him, enjoying the sensation of being filled up by his cock as well as his semen as it trickled out of me.

"You're always going to be my first choice," he rasped against my ear.

"Hmm?" I was too blissed out to know what in the world he was on about.

"Not my parents. No matter what they think, you're always going to be my first choice." He pushed himself up and sat back on his knees, slowly withdrawing his cock from my body.

Once it was out, his fingers circled my hole, catching the trickling semen on them before thrusting them back into my body.

"Oh!" I bucked against him, my nerve-endings working on high gear.

"You're the best thing that's ever happened to me, Ki." Fingers came out, to be replaced by one long, deep thrust of his slowly-softening cock. "You and I are so good together. You're always going to be... My. First. Choice." He emphasised each word with a thrust of his hips.

"Oh, God." I threw a hand over my eyes.

He held my legs spread wide, gripping them at the ankle. I was open and ready for whatever else he wanted to dish me, but he only kept thrusting until he got so soft that it was impossible to continue anymore.

"You are a fucking sex god," I said once he let my legs down on the bed so I could stretch out properly, feeling wonderfully sore and properly shagged.

He barked a laugh. "Hardly that high up."

"Oh, you don't give yourself enough credit." I removed my arm from my eyes and pushed myself up on my elbows so I could look at him.

My come was rubbed all over both our stomachs. His was still trickling out of me and covering his dick, so it was all shiny-looking.

"We should shower. I didn't know we were having sex, so I didn't douche."

I hadn't been uptight about cleaning out properly in the beginning, but back then, we'd been using condoms. Now that we were fucking bare, it was more important than ever.

"Put the sheets in the washer too, less we forget about them entirely."

"Wouldn't want your mum to find them." That was a horrifying thought. Christmas was shaping out to be not a pleasant experience to begin with— wouldn't want to add to it.

"My thoughts exactly." He pulled me up on my knees and flush against him, then kissed me deeply. "Happy Christmas, love."

"It isn't until tomorrow," I pointed out.

"Think of it as your early Christmas gift." His hand slid down my back to cup my arse, squeezing a bit while his index finger slid in-between the crack to slide in my entrance.

"I like these kinds of gifts," I whispered against his lips, pushing my arse out to try and get more of his finger inside.

"I know you do. And I like giving them to you." He grinned.

"Never stop." He thrust his index finger in and out of me, and if he kept this up, I would be ready to go another round in no time.

"Want to move the second round to the shower?"

My thoughts exactly.

"You have no idea just how much I'd like that." I paused, then added with a wide grin, "Sylvester."

He swatted at me, and we stumbled across the hall, still naked and covered in our own bodily fluids.

Thankfully no one had come home early and we went undetected.

So did our rendezvous in the shower; which was faster, dirtier, and louder than our session in bed had been.

Happy Christmas, indeed.

As long as I could have this, I could tolerate disapproving parents and everything else the world wanted to throw at me.

With this, I could take anything.

As long as I had him, everything was possible.

TT lives in Norway and writes about gay men living in Norway. She also occasionally writes about gay men living in the UK, because she loves the UK. Norway might be too cold for her, but TT doesn't like the summer, so she's learned to adapt. TT is happiest in front of her computer, creating emotional stories about men loving other men.

www.ttkove.com
ttkove@gmail.com